THE THIEVES OF SUMMER

THE THIEVES OF SUMMER

Linda Sillitoe

foreword by Cynthia Sillitoe

Signature Books | Salt Lake City | 2014

www.signaturebooks.com

Cover design by Ron Stucki.
Book design by Jason Francis.

18   17   16   15   14   5   4   3   2   1

LIBRARY OF CONGRESS CATALOGING-IN-PUBLICATION DATA

Sillitoe, Linda, 1948-2010, author.
   The thieves of summer / by Linda Sillitoe. — First edition.
      pages cm

   Summary: Set in Salt Lake City at the height of the Great Depression, Linda Sillitoe's last novel opens with three little girls, eleven-year-old triplets, skipping in front of their house across from the park. Unknown to them, the elephant the children of Utah purchased for the circus by donating nickels and dimes goes on late-night strolls with her trainer. They do know that sometimes the elephant escapes and goes on rampages in the neighborhood. The girls' father is a police officer investigating a boy's disappearance. As the case unfolds, the perception of the park changes from a place of freedom to a place to be avoided. The story is loosely based on the exploits of a real live elephant that lived in Salt Lake's Liberty Park a decade before Sillitoe's childhood in the neighborhood..

   ISBN 978-1-56085-227-8 (alk. paper)
1. Salt Lake City (Utah)—Fiction. 2. Depressions—1929—Utah—Fiction.
3. Elephants—Fiction. 4. Missing children—Fiction. 5. Utah—History—
Fiction. I. Title.
   PS3569.I447T48 2013
   813'.54—dc23
                        2013028324

CONTENTS

Foreword

This is a book my mother, Linda Sillitoe, almost didn't live to finish writing. She began it in early 2009. Despite serious and debilitating illnesses, she completed and submitted the manuscript to Signature Books just weeks before her death in April 2010. In this one story, she combined all the phases of her thirty-five-year career: poetry, fiction, true crime, and history.

As she says in the prologue, it is a different story than the one she had expected to write. In her red unlined journal, she sketched out the idea for a novel that would span several generations of one family. She didn't usually talk about projects during their conceptual stage but told me one night at dinner, "I think it's actually going to take place over just one summer."

Mom grew up the daughter of a police officer who eventually left the force to become a salesman, a small-business owner with my grandmother, and then a locksmith. Mom told me that while he was still a cop, he would come home in uniform and toss his cap on the table, then run his fingers through his dark curls. Grandpa's once-thick hair is hard for my generation to imagine, but there are photographs to prove it. If he was in a good mood, he might talk about his day at work, usually tales of crooks who had been tripped up by their own foolishness.

In reality, most cases ended in tragedy, so Grandpa kept the details to himself, the exception being when an investigation became such big news that everyone heard about it. One such case, involving the murder of a young woman, Grandpa solved—not with a gun or a car chase, but by asking the right questions. The second case was the disappearance of a little boy. He was there one moment and gone the next. Without witnesses or an evidence trail, the police couldn't even be sure that he had been kidnapped: he might have just wandered off. But it was all the adults talked about, always in hushed tones so the children wouldn't overhear. This is how, at a very early age, my mother first experienced the irresistible pull of a mystery. While her parents reiterated the usual warnings—don't leave the yard without permission, don't talk to strangers, and don't go into their cars or houses—my mother responded with questions of her own: How could a child vanish? Who would take him? Why?

When no one offered explanations, her curiosity became even more inflamed. While she was lying awake in bed or roller skating on the front porch, she turned the facts over in her mind to see if she could figure out how the pieces fit together. She was an avid newspaper reader, who checked both morning and evening editions for updates on the case. Once she thought she might finally learn something useful when, during a visit from her Aunt Fern, she overheard Fern ask her brother-in-law, "Bob, what do you think happened to that little boy?" Grandpa's reply was too soft for my mother to hear, but it made Fern gasp and recoil.

The boy was never found and the case was left unsolved. My mother grew up and became a poet and fiction writer. At the 1979 International Women's Year meetings in Salt Lake City, amid debate on the proposed Equal Rights Amendment, she asked the right questions and landed an unexpected career as a journalist. Later, that profession changed when she left her job at the newspaper to co-author a true-crime book, *Salamander: The Story of the Mormon Forgery Murders.*

Occasionally she was reminded of the first mystery of her childhood—the boy who had vanished. She meant to ask her father about it, but their conversations usually ended up taking place at family gatherings, where a new generation of children was poised to overhear. She waited too long. When Grandpa suddenly died, she realized she would have to solve the case in a fictional way, based on her intuition and experience as a journalist.

Mysteries weren't the only thing that fascinated my mother at a young age. She loved elephants so much that for her fifth birthday, she told me, she asked for one as a pet. She said her father responded that she could have one if she agreed to clean up after it. Then he gave her an idea of how much shoveling that would entail, saying she would have to pay for its food as well. Since she already faced the weekly dilemma of whether to spend her ten-cent allowance on either paper dolls or drawing paper—but not both—she had to accept the fact that feeding a multi-ton pet would be beyond her means.

Her fascination with elephants never waned, however. As the animals themselves do, her interest grew unfettered so that by the time I was an adult, she had a small library of books on elephants. I borrowed one and found myself just as enthralled. Elephants are extraordinary, magical creatures. Their trunks are so powerful that they can topple a tree with a single motion; with that same trunk, they can delicately lift a newborn calf to its feet and guide its first steps. In a stampede, elephants are an earth-shaking blunder, but when they choose to they can move with silence and grace. They are comical and wise, intuitive and sly, and no, they never forget.

Setting this book in the Liberty Park neighborhood where Mom grew up meant she could include the park's most famous resident, the very-real elephant called Princess Alice. This meant that the novel would have to take place earlier than the 1950s of my mother's childhood. As she began her research, she settled on the year 1938. Soon she found a surprisingly close source when she discovered that her friend of thirty years, Emma Lou Thayne, had spent summers exercising horses in Liberty Park. Emma Lou remembered Princess Alice well. While she never actually chased down the elephant, Mom couldn't resist the image of her friend doing just that. In spite of her assertion that the story's characters are all fictional, I can assure you that Nora is, in fact, Emma Lou Thayne. To those who know her, Emma Lou's adventurous and optimistic spirit is as recognizable as her vocal cadence.

The other characters are mostly fictional, with some exceptions. Mom thought she could disguise her father by making him blond and giving him a Philadelphia childhood, but it is easy to see Grandpa in Evan. Similarly, Evan's wife, Rose, shares my grandmother's skill as a seamstress, her nurturing spirit, and her role as the peacemaker in the family. Mom gave Rose a simpler worldview than Grandma possessed, but I can tell who it is. I also see my Aunt Susan in Annabel, especially Annabel's desire for structure and certainty. Susan and my mom were born just fifteen months apart and were almost like twins in the way they shared memories their younger siblings did not have. While, my mother was writing this story, Susan was battling bone cancer and died just a few months before my mother's death.

To me, there are two more parallels: Carolee's obsession with newspapers, dictionaries, and careful analysis of the facts of the case reveals one side of my mother's personality, while Bethany's characteristics as a dreamer, elephant lover, and occasional rebel represent another.

It was a bittersweet experience for me to work with the publisher through the final editing. I find that my mother is most present for me when I'm reading her writing, but even so, it was daunting deciding which sections needed some clarification and which should be left alone. In any changes we made, I relied heavily on conversations with my mother about writing and editing. I am confident she would approve of this final draft, also that she would be flattered by the complementary visual aspects, including the cover, the running heads, the key icon between scenes, and the section dividers.

This is my mother's last story. I think it is appropriate that it blends her poetic voice, her insight into people, her refusal to look away from the shadows in life, and her belief in ordinary magic—as well as her incredible sense of humor. For all those reasons and more, I am happy to share it with you.

—Cynthia Sillitoe, Ogden, Utah, May 2014.

Prologue

Princess Alice had no intention of relocating, and like most elephants, she meant to have her own way.

I knew nothing of this when I was a child, dwelling in one home or another near Liberty Park in Salt Lake City. Named after Alice Roosevelt, the feisty and admired daughter of President Theodore Roosevelt, the princess munched on green hay all day under tall shady trees, entertaining her visitors and occasionally outraging her neighbors for over two decades.

A few years before Princess Alice was born in India (most likely, but unknown), Salt Lake City purchased Liberty Park from colonizer Brigham Young, the planter of its cottonwood and mulberry trees. By the turn of the twentieth century, Young had died, polygamy had dwindled, and the legislature of Utah Territory had convinced Congress to vote for statehood. Salt Lake City rushed into the new century with electric streetlights all ablaze and set about filling Liberty Park with attractions, including a zoo. Naturally, a zoo needed an elephant, so the search was on.

The problem was that even in 1916 elephants were expensive. Before my parents were born, schoolchildren throughout the city donated pennies and nickels to purchase the elephant for $3,250 from the Sells-Floto Show Company, a circus that later joined the Ringling Brothers empire. For over two decades, Princess Alice not only reigned over Liberty Park but also occasionally strolled through the nearby developing neighborhoods, prompting the construction of a more secure zoo above the valley.

But Princess Alice preferred *not* to relocate. Eventually, she did just that, but it was not her choice.

My father served in the army reserves during the Korean War. Afterward, my parents purchased a red brick cottage near the park where we all attended Mormon church services in the Liberty Ward; I entered kindergarten at Liberty School. At that time, an aged Princess Alice died at the zoo at the mouth of Emigration Canyon. Even so, her stone visage adorned the elephant house, and her name echoed so strongly that I believed her to be one of the trunk-swinging giants we visited there. When my first-grade year ended and, clad in pedal-pushers, we toted sack lunches to Liberty Park, only a small herd of begging deer and a depressed black bear echoed the former zoo's inhabitants amid the birds of what had become Tracy Aviary.

Little did I know that when my family moved directly across the street from the tennis courts, so the swat and plonk of balls filtered through our screens on early summer mornings, our bungalow's earlier occupants had sometimes been roused to the blast of an elephant. If only we teenagers had lazed on our big porch swing a few decades earlier, Princess Alice might have ambled across the street to greet us.

The setting for this story is the summer of 1938. It was an era of contradictions, when kidnapping was rife but shoplifting and child abuse were barely known. It was a time when childhood extended, paychecks shrank, and terror raced across Europe and China. Princess Alice is the novel's sole historical character, and even she has been stretched a bit. I have also transformed her lesser known trainer, Dutch Shider, to meet the needs of the story.

Actually, I intended to write a different novel, although sited near Liberty Park. I kept reading books about elephants, with the feeling I had been tapped on the head by a spirit trunk. Eventually, I pilfered a few items from Dad's old police scrapbook, one concerning a mysterious case he had solved and another case he left for me.

—Linda Sillitoe, 2010

JUNE

one

Nora Taylor expected good fortune from life—even part-time employment at age sixteen during the Great Depression—but had never expected to chase an elephant on horseback.

Each summer, her family spent the summer at their cabin below Brighton Canyon. Luckily for Nora, the man who owned the neighboring cabin also owned the stables on West Temple Street in Salt Lake City. He knew that Nora, a skilled rider, was a responsible teen, and he offered her a job exercising horses. Nora accepted. She was too restless for leisure anyway. She even liked the early morning commute, her older brother at the wheel of the family pickup truck as the sun eased up toward the peaks of the Wasatch Range. Each weekday, while her brother taught tennis in Liberty Park, Nora took the horses out, one at a time, giving each a good run. She'd finish at roughly the same time her brother's classes ended and they would drive back to the canyon before the day's heat set in.

On June 5, 1938, astride a mare named Jackpot, Nora rode down Thirteenth South and turned onto the unpaved circle of Liberty Park. It was deliciously cool, still quiet except for songbirds in the corner fir trees, a few zoo animals rousing themselves toward the south, and the noisome gulls that liked to swoop down to the grass and onto the island in the middle of Liberty Lake. (In Nora's opinion, it was more of a pond.) Once they passed the north gate on Ninth South, Nora signaled a gallop and leaned through the curve, reining in as they passed the tennis courts; she saluted her brother as he taught backhand to a class of youngsters.

As they cantered around the south end of the circle, Nora heard a man shout and saw the elephant, Princess Alice, shove her giant head against the outer fence until, amazingly, the rods bent, then bent farther and snapped. The trainer grabbed his bull hook but was too late, the elephant having pressed her powerful front foot through the torn metal and shouldered her way free. She trumpeted cheerfully and headed east.

Nora instinctively swung Jackpot around to follow, leaving a breadth of open space between them and the elephant. "I'll see if I can head her back," she called over her shoulder.

"Fine, just don't—"

As his words were drowned out in the clatter of hooves, Nora wondered what he meant. *Don't what?* she asked herself. *Don't provoke the elephant? Don't chase it into traffic? Don't kill the stable owner's favorite mare, not to mention her parents' only daughter?*

Traffic was scant that early, but the vision of an elephant, a horse, and its rider colliding with vehicles was too horrid to contemplate. Her own heart drumming, Nora sensed Jackpot's reluctance to pursue such an enormous beast. "Come on, Jackpot, it's just an elephant."

As she drew closer, Nora was fascinated to see how silently Princess Alice traveled, her rear feet landing in the dents her front feet squashed in the wet lawn. Even on grass, the hooves of a running horse struck considerably louder. How odd! Nora felt Jackpot's tension increase and saw Princess Alice glance back warily. Perhaps her caution could be used to everyone's advantage.

Nora clucked and reined Jackpot to the right. If she could move between Princess Alice and the fast-coming intersection of Thirteenth South and Seventh East, maybe she could steer the elephant back. Nora concentrated on drawing parallel with Princess Alice and, staying ten feet to the elephant's right, turned Jackpot slightly inward while maintaining her speed.

Instinctively, Princess Alice edged to her left and gradually, almost casually, completed a large U-turn while dodging the trees and picnic benches. The elephant trotted along steadily as if she quite preferred this encounter with the horse to invading traffic. Nora grinned. They returned at a nonchalant pace to the damaged corral, where Princess Alice headed straight to the barn, knowing it was where she would serve time as punishment for running amok.

Immensely relieved, Hugo Stuka refused to chat with the runaway elephant as he attached her foot chain, secured the outside locks, and went to introduce himself to the girl who had prevented more trouble than she knew. He wished he could give her a medal.

"Nora Taylor, Mr. Stuka," she said. "I'm glad I could help. All of us just love Princess Alice."

"Oh, how I wish that was true." He mopped his forehead and neck with a bandana and offered a worried grin. "The city commission insists that she move to that new Hogle Zoo. One of the commissioners said she's dangerous. A menace to the city, he said. You can see why I can't have her running free. Not again," he added wearily.

"How could he think she's dangerous? She just likes to get some exercise. I take the horses out almost every morning and they never get enough. They ought to let you take Princess Alice for a gallop around the circle sometimes."

Hugo chuckled, disinclined to mention his secret excursions under the full moon, especially to a new acquaintance. "A ride around the circle would be good. Her fans would love a gallop like that, and Princess might get into less trouble back here, that's true."

He pulled a flat silver key from his pocket and showed it to Nora. "This key to the shed went missing for four days. I needed it and knew Princess had done something with it. I couldn't find it anywhere here or in the barn. I even checked at home. No key.

"So I watched her dung in case she had swallowed it. I felt in the upper folds of her trunk, got her to open her mouth, looked between her toes. No key. She knew I was hunting for it, of course. The naughty pickpocket!"

Nora laughed in delight. "Gee whilikers! Where did you find it?"

"Well, yesterday morning I picked up a huge bunch of over-ripe bananas from the market and set them just outside the corral where Princess could see and smell them even from inside her barn. All during her bath, I talked about that key, how if she gave it back she could have all the bananas at once. After I rinsed her off, she put her trunk deep into one of the pockets in her mouth, and out came the key. She set it in my hand, pretty as you please."

"But you had looked in her mouth. You mean she had it inside her mouth all that time?"

"Oh, an elephant's mouth has so many folds and creases,

you never know where it might be hidden—unless she wants it found."

"That's amazing. Horses don't have anything in their mouths but teeth and a tongue. No wonder Princess Alice is such a star. If she has to move to Hogle Zoo, I'm going to miss her." She grinned and tapped Hugo's calloused hand. "Let's persuade the city to allow me to exercise Princess Alice when I come by with horses three times a day—that should fix her wanderlust."

Hugo exhaled and shook his head. "I like the idea but I'm afraid Princess would not like being around a horse. You saw how she avoided yours today."

"Jackpot didn't like being near an elephant either! But you're right. The city wouldn't agree anyway."

"No, they wouldn't. I don't want her moving to that new zoo because I live close by the park, but maybe it would be better for her to live up there in the canyon. The city has grown so much since we first came here twenty-two years ago! That was before you were even born, am I right?"

"Yes," she admitted. Jackpot whinnied and danced impatiently. A companionable rumble answered from inside the barn. "I'd better get back on the job," Nora said, "or I'll roast before I finish. Nice to meet you, Mr. Stuka."

"Oh, call me Hugo. Thank you again, Nora. You saved the day."

He went to re-examine the fence. He had telephoned repairmen, who were already on their way. Maybe a moat would work better, he thought. Would that be safe? Probably the city commissioners would not approve of any expensive changes since they wanted to relocate her anyway.

As Nora turned her steed west on Thirteenth South, a sunbeam scorched the back of her neck. She waved at the character across the street, whom she privately called Pinky because of the shade of his skin, as he watered a scrubby lawn surrounding a small, frame house.

At a nearby bungalow, a heavyset woman pushed a wheelchair down the driveway and across the front lawn, turning it to face the park but drawing it close to a shady willow. The chair held a teen-aged girl who was clearly paralyzed. Nora waved to her too, unconsciously straightening in the saddle, grateful for her body's strength and speed. She urged Jackpot to trot a little faster. Not only did they own the morning, Nora sensed a connection to her future that stretched farther than she could see.

8—⊓

The streets bordering Liberty Park had two narrow lanes each so that when Princess Alice took an unauthorized stroll, her bulk and drift monopolized both lanes. Maybe, Hugo mused as he viewed the damaged corral, she was drawn to the movement of the clotheslines strung outside the pastel cottages on Seventh East when women hung out their weekly wash. Princess would pluck a capacious dress or robe, maybe two, to fling over her head and shoulders. Then she would revel in the limelight amid the crowd of blaring vehicles, cheering youth, and nervous adults. Outside her enclosure, she struck more awe than curiosity, so no one approached her too closely until Stuka arrived with his wooden bull hook. He seldom used it, but every elephant trained as a calf feared the utensil for its propensity to poke tender places.

Princess Alice seemed to know her attraction remained unchallenged in the city. So far Hogle Zoo had only puma cubs, rabbits, birds, and deer on exhibit. Soon they would add seals and foxes. But at Liberty Park, amid the paddle boats, the towering slippery slides and swings, and the classic Allen-Herschel carousel tinkling its tunes across the general tumult, large crowds sought out the elephant enclosure.

Hugo opened the barn and prepared Princess Alice's belated morning bath. His relief at having her back safe and sound mixed with his impatience at her feistiness. She was as exasperating as she was valuable, being the only elephant for at least a thousand miles and the only one in North America who had repeatedly calved in captivity. Still, Hugo knew that millions of years of wild blood flowed through her arteries. Naturally she tolerated zoo life as restlessly as even a well-behaved child would tolerate captivity. She obeyed her keeper most of the time and was friendly to everyone else, with the occasional exception, and that camaraderie, Hugo mused, was more than any of them deserved.

He had not expected trouble today. When he first opened the barn, she had seemed calm enough, just shaking her ears as usual and squealing *Where are my oats?* He had noticed that she had chuckled deep in her throat and shifted impatiently while he clipped open a fresh bale of hay, then the instant he turned to unlock the cabinet to get the pitchfork, she had brushed past him and left. By the time he picked himself up, she had gotten far enough to require a chase, though this time, for once, not by Hugo.

Regardless of her naughty behavior, she was hungry now and needed to be fed. He filled the first tub of the fifty pounds of grain she would eat in a day and the first bucket of the forty gallons she would drink, then he threw the back doors wide before shoveling out her used bedding hay.

"In one end, out the other," he muttered. Soon a truck

and two strapping lads from the garden division would arrive and remove the hill of manure that stood behind the barn. An elephant could eliminate a hundred pounds or more of manure in one good poop, and the grounds keepers kept the park green and flowers vibrant with it.

"Maybe Mother Nature will favor us with a spring breeze today, Princess, just about the time your loving public starts to arrive." She fanned her left ear to acknowledge she had heard, but poop was his concern, breakfast hers.

During the summer, children appeared all day, accompanied by mothers or sitters and joined lately by unemployed men too, discouraged enough to give up hunting for jobs. Hugo could spot them by their dejected posture, their ambling walk, and sometimes—if he looked—a look of disbelief in their eyes. He preferred keeping an eye on the children. Some of the more bedraggled ones reminded Hugo of himself at their age.

As a boy, he and his family had left Europe for a better life, but at sea, typhoid spread through the ship's steerage section and he arrived in Manhattan as an orphan. He found the city's zoos held fascinating animals, as well as an easy chance to snatch the fruit and vegetables the animals ignored. Gradually he formed an attachment with the trainer, Rijay Shikar, who had accompanied several elephant calves from northeastern India in 1900. That was when Hugo met the princess.

By age fourteen Hugo had learned enough about preparing feed and shoveling manure to be granted an apprenticeship with Rijay, which for Hugo meant regular meals. A few months later, after the typical elephant gestation of two years, Princess Alice dropped her first calf. Initially she seemed confused, but quickly she became a devoted mother, while retaining her regal manner. Much to Shikar's amusement, she would only let Hugo near her calf. The little elephant was predictably named Raja, which meant prince. Hugo had helped him gain his footing and find Princess's breast the first time he nursed. The boy felt a bit embarrassed when he realized that a mother elephant's anatomy resembled a woman's more than a cow's.

Talking or singing in a low voice, Shikar bathed the elephants and taught Hugo how to move a loofah into the deep folds of their hairy skin, checking for insect bites or scrapes. He laughed at Hugo when Raja learned how to drench him with his little floppy trunk. Month after month, Hugo learned not only how to bathe an elephant but how to judge its mood, spot ailments, and pick up signs of communication. All around him the elephants conducted their own uncanny rumbles, missing nothing in their environment.

As they worked, Shikar explained how females developed in the wild, tolerating the presence of their own male calves only until the boys reached sexual maturity in their teens. After that, the males were forced to roam in small bachelor groups or alone, becoming testy during sexual *musth* when they would visit a herd to find females ripe for breeding. Herds rarely developed in captivity because calves of both genders were usually sold quickly. Initially Princess Alice was fortunate, for the traveling circus that owned her also wanted Raja. Hugo went along as a *mahout*, Hindi for an elephant rider.

There were hard years ahead spent on the road with the circus's whistle-stop tour through over half the states. Somewhere in Indiana, the decision was made to sell Raja. Hugo kept Princess busy that day so she wouldn't notice her calf's absence. She walked in the parade, helped erect the big-top tent, performed as a harmonica-blowing clown, and hosed out a burning prop. She closed with three other elephants who had learned to waltz decorously beneath showgirls clad in blue satin and sequins. Even when the evening crowd dispersed, Princess helped break down the circus. She was visibly tired as she boarded the train to munch her midnight meal of over-ripe potatoes and wilted carrots. When she discovered that her baby was missing, Hugo was there to comfort her, sleeping behind a partition and trying, but failing, to reassure her as the train clattered into Illinois.

Princess Alice lived most of every year, like Hugo, sleeping to the rhythm of the rails, always short on rest. She mated in Florida when the circus wintered there, eventually bearing a female calf. Once weaned, the comical Paulette was sold. When Princess mated again, she turned wary. With Shandara, her third offspring, the mother trained a dark eye on the circus manager each time he admired her baby. Remarkably, she held him responsible when, during a three-day run in Michigan, Shandara disappeared. No matter the manager's offers of tangerines or even pineapples, she began extending her trunk in his direction to blast her fury every time he came by, alarming the other animals. The manager got the message and ceased visiting her.

To Hugo's surprise, Princess mated again that winter. As the circus loaded and she once again let her hostility toward the manager flare, Hugo suspected that she might be pregnant and added a rear stake in the barn; he freed her only for short stints when they needed her work. He knew elephants could sniff out a particular human in a village as easily as they could lift a peanut from the circus ring. Consistent vegetarians, they did not kill for food or indiscriminately but were known to seek out and literally obliterate a known offender, even years after a suspected crime. The scent of alcohol seemed to increase their fury, Hugo learned from Shikar, and the manager liked brandy in the evening. The train rattled west, the manager keeping to the office car near the engine while he sought a buyer for the prized elephant. Had he known about the possible calf, which Hugo intentionally did not mention, the final selling price would have been higher.

The zoo in Liberty Park was small, but the park itself extended a few square blocks. It was not far from the granite temple five blocks west and nine blocks to the north. Hugo had settled in without any trouble, and Princess accepted the new routine without complaint. Once she was fed and bathed, Hugo would let her into the double-fenced enclosure while he worked nearby. He kept a keen eye on the children who were too young to be left alone near an elephant. Recently he had noticed one who seemed to be a potential troublemaker. In fact, the child's whitish curls caused Hugo to mistakenly assume it was a little girl. One day when the police came by with a photograph, they asked if he had seen the boy, they said, who was now missing. They had many questions.

"It crossed my mind that the child might be lost," Hugo told the officers. "It was too young to wander around alone."

"Did he seem distressed?"

"Not at all. Of course, all the children enjoy Princess Alice. I was busy making sure no one came too close. Not even double fences totally protect kids or elephants, you know?"

"Why did you notice this child in particular?" the shorter officer asked sharply.

"Like I said, she—I mean, he—was such a little kid to be alone and was kind of acting up, like he might try to feed something to Princess or crawl inside the enclosure. I always have to watch out for that. Anyway, he was not holding a mother's hand, which is rare."

The officers wrote down Hugo's full name and home address and abruptly left. *Is it my foreign accent that makes them suspect me?* he asked himself.

His native Czechoslovakia was falling apart, as was all of Europe. He did not feel attached to his homeland any more than he did to America, but people saw him as a stranger. Being an elephant trainer was a misunderstood occupation. Did the police think he eyed children all day? He would like to see those condescending officers fetch a gallon of cool water for Princess Alice, or heft a shovel for that matter.

Feeding, shoveling, grooming, exercising, more feeding, more shoveling—that was Hugo's life. If Princess had her own herd, she would manage such things for herself, dividing up the work among her daughters and other female relatives. Elephants lived as long as seventy years, all the while their brains and bodies continuing to grow. In a city park, one giant elephant was enough for the limited enclosure, especially if she possessed Princess Alice's intelligence and feisty independence.

Maybe in Emigration Canyon she would be happier. But no, Hugo tried not to think about it. Sometimes it seemed that Princess read his mind, maybe just as easily as he might read a magazine. He could also tell what she was thinking. *See, now she's swaying a bit.* He reached for the largest grooming brush, knowing that the stroking would settle them both.

⚷

Across the street from the park, Sol Niessen turned off the short lawn hose, rubbed his wet hands over his rosy face and sweaty hair, and settled comfortably into his metal porch chair. He opened a bag of potato chips. Armed with binoculars on his screened porch, he could see virtually everything that went on around the south end of Liberty Park. His view provided daily entertainment. He watched the girl with the brunette ponytail who brought horses for exercise. It was a miserably hot business even in the morning, he thought.

In a decade when jobs were hard to find, he came to see his spot on the porch as his place in the world. He liked that it did not require a uniform or wardrobe and no advanced education, and it was all possible with just the small annuity his dead mother had left him. Like her, he loved relaxing on the screened porch, feeling in contact with the outside world and remaining almost invisible, just a shadow occasionally waving at passers-by. He was seldom bothered by the tall, competitive fellows or pretty females he had barely spoken to in high school. They married one another and supplied the city with lovely young creatures who appeared now and then across the street from him.

Maybe I'm the pied piper in that fairytale Ma used to read. The little brats look up to me—even if they don't have to look up very far.

He chuckled at his own joke about his height and slowed his consumption of chips so he could savor their salt. He loved the curiosity the kids showed when he hinted at something special, their look of wonder when he showed them something that defied their experience. Eventually most became squirmy, embarrassed, uncomfortable, but he tried to put them at ease. After all, he could use the pills his mother had left behind, prescriptions he had stockpiled for a time after her death. Or if a child became difficult, he offered an exciting ride on one of the new buses that had recently replaced the trolleys. If he walked a child to the stop on Seventh East and waited until a bus came in sight, he never had trouble with that particular child again.

A dog would find its way back to my house. Even a cat, and I hate cats, Sol said to himself. *But brats—they don't come back. Not once, not ever.*

Through the screen door behind him, Sol heard a muffled pounding. "Somebody's awake already," he singsonged to himself and sighed.

two

South of Liberty Park on Sherman Avenue, the Flynn triplets were weeding the backyard vegetable garden under duress. The plot was irrigated every night by a trickle from the hose through a clever system of furrows dug by their father and older brother, but the hot and tedious work of weeding was assigned to the girls. (The triplets had noticed that their sister, Joyce, managed to escape the task somehow. It was unjust, but she was four years older, a fact she never let them forget.)

At last, they finished up, washed their hands and their t-strap sandals at the front tap, then shared the wood swing that hung from the huge cottonwood tree in the center of the backyard.

"It's time to plan our summer projects," Annabel announced.

To their annoyance, the park was officially banned except with specific permission because of the little boy who had gone missing. Yet for imaginative eleven-year-olds, unafraid of the pitfalls that might endanger younger children, intrigue lurked all around.

"You're right. I'm going to figure out what happened to that Frankie Stuart. He was a ninny when I tended him,"

Carolee said. "I'll bet he wasn't even near the park and someone clobbered him because he was whining."

"I'll see if Hugo knows anything," Bethany shrugged. If she didn't forget, that is. She kept a host of elephant questions buzzing in her brain until she neared the zoo, and then the questions multiplied until she couldn't ever remember the ones she had wanted to ask most.

"You've given me an idea. My project can be finding Pearlann Jones," Annabel said. "Maybe she's chained in her basement, drooling and gnashing her teeth. Remember that Sunday when she stood by the church steps, all giggly and handing out her wedding invitations? Of course," she added thoughtfully, "that *did* save on postage stamps"

"She probably just went back to that special school in American Fork," Carolee drawled. "Anyway, she's older than Glenn and he's nineteen. Grown-ups can take off anytime they want."

"She doesn't seem all that grown-up," Annabel protested. "Besides, her parents would know if she went back to that school. I still have my invitation under the bed. I heard Papa tell Mama that her wedding day was when her parents lost track of her. So the invitation is a clue."

Bethany gazed at her sisters, not for the first time noticing how alike her sisters' dark hair was, yet resisting the way their minds worked in tandem. "Don't you think missing people are projects for Papa and the other detectives rather than for children?"

"Kids can find out things the police can't," Carolee retorted, "because nobody notices them, and some people don't want to talk to the police."

"The bad guys *shoot* at police!" Annabel interrupted. The

triplets greatly admired their father's scarred arm but did not relish being inflicted by a similar wound.

"Nobody shoots children, though" Carolee observed. "Besides, we have lots of time, the whole summer practically. We ought to play street soccer every morning and work on our projects after that." For a moment they felt rich in the summer's infinite possibilities.

"Except for our chores! And practicing the piano," Annabel sighed. "And I'm tired of having to share Joyce's old bicycle among the three of us. If we don't stay busy, Mama might make us sell vegetables like Thelma and Nancy Ryan have to do." She shuddered at the thought of it. "Even Mrs. Loydean around the corner has a sign up for cupcakes and rolls."

"Mmm, I'd like a cupcake," Bethany said.

"For a nickel!"

"It's bad enough that we have to practice piano when Marianne's not even in town and we won't have lessons again until school starts," Carolee said.

"Because Marianne took the job at the girls' camp. Otherwise we'd have lessons through the summer." It was a horrible thought. (The sisters rather liked the dance classes offered in a neighbor's converted garage, so no one complained about those.) "I still think finding missing people is too hard," Bethany continued. She thought about it for a second. "I think, instead of that, I'm going to figure out how to make Princess Alice spray water on her visitors."

"She does that already," Annabel said.

"Not on command," Bethany retorted.

"I'd like a shower bath," Carolee sighed. "It would feel good today. Maybe later Mama will let us have a water fight with the hose."

Annabel shook her head. "Po-li-o," she sang out. "Everyone knows the president got polio because he got chilled. Besides, you'll just remind her to make us rest this afternoon like babies. I really don't understand how a nap is supposed to keep anyone from getting sick. Let's ask her if we can go over to the park and jump rope where it's shadier. I'll see if we can buy an ice cone from that guy who parks his cart on the corner."

Their mother gave permission but without any nickels. It was just as well since the vendor was nowhere in sight. "Before we jump rope, let's check on Princess Alice," Bethany suggested. "Maybe she got loose again." They crossed Thirteenth South carefully and then broke into a run, Carolee twirling her jump rope overhead like a lasso. The elephant was not visible, but Bethany thought she heard Princess Alice grumbling.

"She has to stay in the barn for a while," Hugo told them. "We have to get the fencing fixed again."

Sure enough, several men were working with metal slats and heavy wire in the far corner. "How far did she go this time?" Carolee asked.

"Not too far. A girl who exercises horses brought her back."

"I wish I had been here," Bethany said. "Princess Alice is one of my favorite people, but I've never even touched her."

Her sisters laughed, but Hugo nodded. "I know what you mean, Bethany. As a matter of fact, she's my best girl, next to my wife, of course."

"Does your wife know," Carolee cracked, "how big your girlfriend is?"

Bethany flushed at the thought of maybe being Hugo's third best girl.

The triplets performed a running hop with their jump ropes as they headed in the direction of home, chanting

"Prin-cess Al-ice in Li-ber-ty Park, munch-es ba-na-nas 'til
way after dark." Technically, Bethany was not sure whether
her second line was true, for they always had to return home
for supper before it got dark, but they had taken the elephant
bananas and Hugo had not immediately fed them to her.
Bethany daydreamed that some day Princess Alice would
cross Thirteenth South and gallivant far enough south to cut
through their backyard.

"If that behemoth comes in our yard, I'll shoot her," Papa
once thundered at the supper table when Princess Alice had
wandered out, but the triplets just laughed. Papa made similar
threats toward Santa Claus and the Easter Bunny.

It was from her father that Bethany got her light-gold hair,
while the other triplets had their mother's good-looking Irish
black hair. Her father would never say so, but Bethany sensed
he thought of his children as being in two groups, the older
two, Glenn and Joyce, followed by the twins plus Bethany. For
herself, the family teamed as Papa-Mama (Evan-Rose), Glenn-
Joyce, Annabel-Carolee, and Bethany. She couldn't decide if
she liked being solitary or not.

In her favorite daydream, Bethany imagined Princess Alice
not only arriving in their yard but Papa, instead of shooting
her, inviting her in. Unafraid, Bethany would approach the
huge animal, pet her knees and kiss her trunk, and let the
elephant wrap her trunk around and swing her up high onto an
impossibly broad neck for a triumphant ride back to the park.

Bethany's sisters loved Princess Alice too, but their wishes
were less exotic. On the Saturday before the last day of fifth
grade, they had voted to celebrate their eleventh birthday by
viewing the movie *Quintuplet Land* in a downtown theater.
After feasting on fried chicken and birthday cake that evening,

the triplets had opened presents and learned why their mother's sewing machine had been humming late into the night. Each one received a new sundress with matching shorts. "We can wear them to Saltair!" Annabel suggested.

"And on the rides at Lagoon," Bethany said.

"And back to see *Quintuplet Land* again," Carolee added.

Their parents exchanged glances but refrained from mentioning their financial constraints.

"I like the cool, refreshing colors," their sister Joyce had commented, quick to remind everyone that she had a sense for fashion because of her part-time job at the ZCMI department store.

As usual, the background color for the sundresses varied even though their design and paper-doll print were the same. Annabel's was predominately pink, with blue for Bethany and mint green for Carolee. The triplets flung their arms around their mother's neck, then squeezed back into the overstuffed chair for more presents.

Smiling graciously, Joyce presented each sister with a tissue-wrapped string of faux pearls she had snatched from the sale table at Notions. They thanked her and traded them around to match the pearls with their dresses, Carolee settling for plain white and the others opting for the silver or pink varieties. Their brother Glenn unceremoniously handed each of them a Milky Way bar, which they happily set aside for later.

Also, Rose had monogrammed a set of new underpants for each girl. On one set, she had embroidered *Carolee* in blue above the left leg opening. For Annabel, she had stitched the days of the week in pastel colors; Bethany's set had the days embroidered in a uniform spring green. When they saw the varieties, everyone laughed, knowing Annabel would meticulously match her underwear to the day, while Bethany would deliberately mix them up.

"Just so I can tell whose is whose when I fold the wash," Rose joked, her green eyes sparkling, "or even better, *you* fold the wash," she told them, shooting Evan a joyful glance. *Imagine, the triplets are eleven!* she seemed to say. Evan's eyes were also suspiciously bright.

Next the girls opened sturdy book bags sewn in yellow, aqua, and red twill to aid their ventures to the public library. "Twenty-one books to read every week," Bethany said, "assuming we read each other's choices." It really wasn't fair that the librarian limited the number of books someone could check out based only on her age. Worse, still, they could only choose from the children's section.

"We'll try to get you there every week," their mother said, "but these bags ought to help you if you take the bus. If you did, you could browse longer."

"That's a good idea," Bethany said, "Even if I can't check out books about elephants from the adult section. I could at least look through those big books."

"Reference books, you mean," her father said, then asked, "Have you really read all the elephant books that they have for kids?"

Bethany nodded.

Annabel bounced up and down, indicating her desire to continue opening presents. Excitement rose as she tore the wrapping, the Sunday funny papers actually, from a stack of five books that all had cut-out dolls featuring the Dionne Quintuplets. She fanned the books into a set and squealed, "One book for each quint!" Tanned hands reached out and compared the books.

Now, as they strolled home from the park, Annabel again

had paper dolls on her mind. "Let's play Dionnes next," she said. "I think we should have a belated party for the quintuplets' fourth birthday."

"Their fourth birthday was our eleventh birthday," Carolee reminded them, never tiring of their connection to the famed quintuplets. "Just think, all of them are identical, but not necessarily to each other. Annette and Marie are twins and the others are triplets," she said, remembering that detail from the movie.

"That's what their doctor thinks," Bethany said, feeling decidedly un-identical. "But how does he know? At least the Dionnes didn't get named alphabetically like we did."

"A good thing since Yvonne would have to wait for twenty-four other babies to be born," Carolee quipped.

"I wonder if in real life their dresses match like they did in the movie," Annabel mused.

"Maybe when Papa's vacation comes in August we can all drive to Canada to see them," Carolee suggested as they cut through the alley to their backyard.

"But August is when Princess Alice might have to move to Hogle Zoo," Bethany offered. "We definitely don't want to miss that. Hugo is working with her on some new tricks to prepare for her big show. I think Princess prefers being *here*, near us."

"She's a lot smarter than those dumb city leaders," Carolee groused. "Didn't Hugo say the zoo celebrated Princess Alice's golden birthday back when she was really only forty-six?"

"He thinks so," Bethany answered, "but it's hard to be sure."

"The city commission might take away Papa's vacation days because of the stupid Depression," Annabel said.

"Why do they say it's the *great* Depression?" Carolee asked. "I don't see what's so great about it. Wait—listen."

A pause. "A plane!" Annabel confirmed. They scooted into the open portion of their yard and stared into the sky to locate the tiny silver cross, barely visible but headed toward the overhead sun.

"Someday I'm going to travel on a plane," Carolee said.

Gazing at her sister, Bethany grasped that eventuality and felt lonely. "I have dibs on the first swing," she called. "It's too hot to go upstairs to our room."

"Well, it sounds like Joyce is practicing the piano," Annabel said. "Let's be alphabetical, so I'll be first after her."

Resettled on his screened porch, Sol Niessen had watched the girls skip rope toward him and then continue down Sixth East. He strained to pick up a name, but they were chanting some jump-rope nonsense. The blond girl was a real prize, he could see. He had watched her before going to and from the park, but today he had decided she was the one.

She was tanned a light gold shade and slim and athletic looking, balanced on the cusp of little girlhood and the messy terrain of puberty. Left alone, she would become a woman. He recoiled at the thought of his mother's headaches and cramps and the obnoxious odor that lingered in the bathroom; this girl, he thought, this blond beauty, need not ever suffer such a vulgar fate as hormonal change. He would seek her identity and rescue her. Patience would be part of the thrill.

A lack of patience could foul things up. He already had proof of that in the storage space between the kitchen ceiling and the pitched roof. He had to crawl under the beams to the outer edge to open the small side windows and hammer them in an open position, about two inches exposed for fresh air but

30 not enough to crawl out of. His old cot in the center of the attic was positioned where he could stand up without bumping his head. The access above the kitchen was hard for him to reach, but once in the attic, his short height was an asset. Good thing, too, that he was wiry and muscular enough to shuttle furniture crates over to the wall opposite the bed.

With everything in place, he stretched away the kinks in his legs and leaned out over the porch steps looking for company.

Detective Evan Flynn was hardly surprised to find himself roped into the Frankie Stuart case. He was relieved he wasn't being considered as a primary investigator. He had experience from another case involving a missing kid from Liberty Park. Well, Pearlann Jones was not really a kid, but was a mentally retarded young adult. Since her family lived in Evan's Mormon ward, his boss thought it made sense to assign him. It was interesting that Brother and Sister Jones seemed more distraught over Pearlann's disappearance than four-year-old Frankie's mother was about him. Frankie's mother seemed to have found a source of serenity in a liquor bottle.

In forty minutes his shift would end, so he started to catch up on paperwork. He put a form in the typewriter and began to peck out answers to basic questions, but his thoughts wandered. Truth be told, there seemed to be as many drunken moms in Salt Lake as there had been in Philadelphia. Mormons seemed to cling together, but in the end the same bad things happened in their neighborhoods, he thought.

His big-city parents had sometimes, but not always, taken the family in the car on Sundays on an hour-long trip to reach the building the Mormons shared with several small businesses. When Evan and his only church buddy, Kelly, had hopped a train west after graduating from high school, they had seen the cities and farms spanning the Great Plains for the first time, and climbing into the Rockies it was surprising to see how much open land there was. Evan noted the greater occurrence of steeples on the western side of the mountains.

In Salt Lake City, Kelly's grandparents had taken them in and introduced them to a police officer who had helped them get started in the police department. Kelly later took a job with the post office, but Evan liked the challenge of police work. He enjoyed sifting through clues, working out motives, and seeing the puzzle pieces fit together. It could be frustrating and even maddening, but rewarding too.

If Evan had remained in Philadelphia, he likely would have married a girl from high school and would not have given much thought to her religion unless she had brought it up. It didn't work that way in Salt Lake. He and Kelly went to a church dance one night where Evan met Rose. It was her looks and vivacity that first attracted him, but after a couple of foxtrots, he became fascinated by the way she thought.

Only halfway aware of it, he had grown up asking "why?" and "why not?" Rose asked "who" first—not only whether he was Mormon but also who his family was. Thanks to polygamous grandparents, she was related to half the residents of Utah in intricate ways she easily tracked, but that still confused Evan. Next she asked "when," "how," "how much," and "where," roughly in that order. "Why" was rarely topical to Rose. Things were as they were; they were expected to continue that way into the eternities. To Evan, this perspective seemed as exotic as his "why" and "why not" attitude did to Rose.

Tonight they would likely miss the opportunity to talk very

32   much. He would be home for dinner but then out again to help conduct a night search for Frankie Stuart. *Or at least for his body,* Evan thought, then winced with guilt. It was too soon to think that way, he thought. For now, Frankie was still a missing child and presumed to be alive.

three

Carolee found the evening newspaper tucked behind a cushion of the big blue sofa. "Who stuck the newspaper back here!" she demanded. If Carolee, who spent all day awaiting the evening newspaper's arrival, did not bring it in from the front porch herself, it was usually lying open somewhere in the living room. She suspected a tease from Joyce, but as soon as she saw the front page, she knew the *why* and probably the *who* of the misplaced paper. It was clearly Rose who had gone out of her way to, not exactly hide, but secure the paper in an inconspicuous space. She hated seeing her children being exposed to dark, seamy events. It wasn't easy to shelter their innocence when there was a police officer in the home.

Carolee pored over the A-1 story on Frankie Stuart's supposed abduction with such intensity that Bethany and Annabel soon squeezed in at either elbow. "It's a blurry photograph," Annabel said. "If we can barely recognize him, how is anyone else supposed to?"

"There's not much information either," said Bethany. "I guess they don't know much yet."

"Papa just drove up," Carolee reported, glancing out the

front window. "Maybe he can tell us more," she said while flopping down onto the floor with the local section.

Their father had not so much as tossed his hat onto the dining room table and placed his gun belt onto the highest cupboard than he solicited information from *them*. When was the last time any of them had seen Frankie Stuart? he wanted to know. Not for quite a while, they decided.

"It's not like we play with four-year-olds," Annabel said.

"Especially not annoying ones," Carolee muttered.

"Have you seen anyone you don't know hanging around the neighborhood?" No.

"Has anyone invited you inside?" No.

"Has anyone invited you inside a car?" No.

"Or acted strange in any way?" No.

"Really, Papa, we're not little kids," Carolee huffed.

"What about someone like that elephant trainer? Has he ever made you feel uncomfortable or tried to separate you?"

"No!" Bethany left for a glass of water and blinked back tears. Hugo was so kind. How could Papa suspect him of hurting a child? In the kitchen, her mother gave her a quick, wordless hug.

Mama always knows when I hurt, Bethany thought as she struggled to compose herself.

Letting go of Bethany, Rose stepped into the dining room and called, "Dinner will be ready soon."

"Good," Evan called back. "We're launching another search in a while."

His voice sounded so weary that Bethany decided to forgive him. She rejoined her sisters and saw her father sitting silently with his ankles crossed, an arm flung over his eyes.

"What are *abrasions?*" Carolee asked from her spot on the parlor floor, the paper spread out before her.

"Scrapes or burns, like a rug burn," her father mumbled. "Like skinning your elbows or knees on the asphalt at school. You asked me last night."

"No, last night I asked about lacerations and internal injuries." Carolee had only recently learned that when there was a photograph of a wrecked car on B-1, it meant there would be an article with more details in that section of the paper.

"Hurry up, Carolee." Annabel hated hearing about wrecks because it made her worry. A hint of catastrophe only burnished her sister's interest in confronting the grisly. "I'm tired of seeing articles about 'petite flower girls' and 'veils of sheerest illusion' on the back page," she said.

"You've got the national news," her father said. "See what FDR is doing lately. Maybe Glenn can get work painting a mural or something. Or I can get a second job as a historian."

"Reading about FDR is too much like school," Annabel sighed, handing the section to her father. "I did at least six reports on him."

"I did my last report on Princess Juliana from Holland," said Carolee. "I wish I'd been named Juliana."

"No, I want to be Juliana," Annabel said. "It's the best name in the world."

"I'll call you *both* Juliana if you'll call me Juliana," Bethany proposed. All three dissolved into giggles.

Their father ducked behind the open newspaper. "Rose did you know this?"

Rose, setting a pitcher of ice water on the dining room table, looked up inquiringly. "Did I know what?"

"For every tax dollar we send to FDR, he sends back seven to Utah for relief efforts. We must be harder hit than Mississippi."

"That's Juliana's fault," Carolee said, and the three were off again.

"Who is Juliana?" Rose asked as the telephone rang.

"That's Juliana calling," Bethany said.

"No, Juliana, it's not her at all. I'm Juliana."

Shaking his head, Evan picked up the receiver, motioning to his daughters to calm down. Listening in, Annabel's eyes brightened.

"It's about Pearlann Jones," she whispered. The three appeared to read avidly, silently, while they all listened to their father make sympathetic sounds and offer reassurance.

"Even so," he wound up, "you'd be surprised how often we find young ladies like your daughter not really lost at all. They move in with a friend, maybe find some work, and forget to tell their families what's going on."

After promising to keep looking, he hung up, and Carolee pretended not to have eavesdropped. "When Juliana gets married," she teased, pointing at Annabel. "She'll have a huge flower girl, not petite at all. A *gigantic* flower girl."

"And, you, Juliana, will wear a veil of inky black." Annabel seized the local section, even as Bethany slipped away, leaving Carolee without anything to read. She studied the outside pages of the national news even as her father read the inside pages. She pondered the way the articles fit so precisely together around the photographs. Who planned it all? she wondered.

Suddenly a thought made Carolee smile and turn back to her sister. "I know! We'll have a double wedding and look perfectly stunning; but we'll parade down the aisle with circus freaks!"

"Not everyone can be a Juliana," said Annabel with mock primness.

"There isn't an aisle to walk down in the temple," their mother said, dropping a kiss on Evan's head and then perusing the front page. "Isn't that horrid Hitler man ever going to stop gobbling up countries?"

"Not until someone stops him," Evan sighed. "I wonder if the line is drawn at Poland. The last thing Europe needs is another Great War, and I'd hate to see us pulled in all over again. Utah always sends more than its share of soldiers."

"I don't think Roosevelt would let the U.S. get involved again. Not after the last one," Rose's voice trembled. She had lost two cousins in the Great War.

Evan offered a reassuring smile but muttered as she turned away, "Unless FDR notices war is the biggest public works program ever invented." Pondering his son of military age, Evan glanced up to find that his daughters were now slow-stepping around the living room, sheets of newspaper draped like veils over their heads.

"Idiots," muttered their sister, Joyce, snatching and reassembling the sections. Her hand tingled to swat her sisters' behinds, but they were too old and she was far too refined. "The table is set, if anybody cares," she said. A new gold pendant dangled under her blouse between her breasts. She turned away to touch it and felt serene.

"Dinner smells done," Rose said. "Where's Bethany? You little brides hunt her up, and then all three of you wash your hands. Don't go in the alley while you're looking," she called after them.

"That's absurd," Carolee whispered as they jumped down the back steps, calling "Ju-li-annn-a!"

38   Joyce and Glenn routinely cut through the alley without being scolded. And of course, the alley was where they found Bethany riding Joyce's old bicycle down the middle. The triplets felt that being deprived of three shining bicycles of their own was a bitter pill. They knew better than to complain, but sometimes the thought of whizzing along in tandem was nearly too much to bear.

"Well, Princess Juliana, have you been visiting Princess Alice?" Annabel asked archly, insinuating their power to tell tales.

Bethany shook her head. She handed each a penny-sized Tootsie Roll. "More at bedtime, Juliana," she announced. "Here you go, Juliana."

Chocolate leaked from the corners of their mouths as they pulled out their chairs at the table. In the interest of peace during supper, Rose pretended not to notice. "No more Juliana," she said firmly, and dinner began.

Around the block, sixteen-year-old Lara Schatz could tell no one of the frightening things her brother Gunther wrote her from Munich, where he worked in Heinrich Himmler's office. Even if she could still speak, even if she had friends, probably no one would believe her. She thought of her friends and relatives in Germany and wondered if they realized what was going on under the Nazis. Didn't anyone have the knowledge and the courage to speak out? According to Gunther, doing so was hopeless and too dangerous by far.

After their leftist parents had died in an auto accident—on a surprisingly dry and uncrowded stretch of road outside Munich—dark-eyed Lara, age ten, had been able to emigrate with her aunt. During their voyage, Lara had begun tripping

over shadows, and by the time they docked in New York
her right arm had grown awkward. (Fortunately, she was
determinedly left-handed, which had greatly frustrated her
teachers in German classrooms.) Manhattan doctors diagnosed hysterical paralysis with hope it might improve.

Not even Amelia Schatz's constant kindness and care could
heal her niece, however, as a train carried them west. By the
time they reached doctors at the University of Utah's teaching
hospital, Lara had lost most of the sight in her right eye and
her speech was growing slurred. Her feet seemed not to hear
her brain's commands, let alone the doctor's directions.

Amelia reported the initial diagnosis, but the neurologist
had shrugged. "That's one way of describing this mystery illness.
It's a disease of the central nervous system, we think, but quite
different from polio. Usually it doesn't strike children as hard or
disable them. Maybe she was vulnerable due to her recent loss."

Lara still had sight and skill on her left side, and she
treasured these remnants of her life. In settling into her aunt's
home near Liberty Park, she carried a sketchbook with her
as her constant companion. Of course, she still missed her
parents and Gunther.

Blond, blue-eyed Gunther had not been allowed to emigrate. Almost immediately after the dual funeral, he had been
named Himmler's ideally Nordic godchild. He was not the first
or last boy to be quasi-adopted by the Reichsfuhrer S.S. Indeed,
Himmler was famous for surrounding himself with Nordic boys.

Once an outgoing youth, Gunther's tongue had been virtually stilled by the shock of losing his family at age fourteen.
As he studied history and race theory in Nazified classrooms,
he deliberately gave correct but monosyllabic answers to the
teacher's sharp questions. His parents had hated this tripe,

he knew, but he feared the teacher's stout pointer and Herr Himmler's scorn. Obedience was paramount; independent thought, not so much. He cast himself in a blunted mold and, in miniature script, poured out his soul to Lara in the States, taping shut that page and concealing it in a conventional letter to his aunt. He knew his sister was ill, but he couldn't resist writing the truth to the only person who might understand.

Hugo Stuka worked an hour past quitting time waiting for the zoo manager to go home. While he bided his time, he meticulously inspected the repairs to the fencing. "You see what you put me through," he grumbled in the direction of the princess as he wheeled the dung cart out the narrow rear door. Changing the conversation to the manure, he estimated "about a ninety-pound load this time, Princess. You must be feeling quite relieved," he said. Like most elephants in captivity, she was trained to spare her public's sensibilities by defecating in private.

Now she offered a friendly rumble.

At least the disappearance of a neighborhood child had shifted the zoo manager's attention away from the rambunctious elephant, for every inch of the park was being searched and all the park employees questioned. A big urban park with all its varied attractions provided a number of ways for a child to go missing. Rumor had it the police would drag Liberty Lake tomorrow.

"Here's the thing about escaping, Princess. You restrict your options when you take escapades outside the park." He paused momentarily by the door to see if Mr. Hill's dark blue Buick was still parked by the small frame office near the pond. It was. He finger-combed his thick, graying hair and patted it down firmly.

"You think you won't be moved to that big new zoo above the city," he muttered, shaking feed grain into the bin. "You think good old Hugo will always take care of you. Good old Hugo, who freed you from the traveling circus so you could live the next forty years being pampered in a shady park with lots of room." He squelched a surge of guilt, thinking about how Princess at least had once had contact with other elephants in the circus.

He drew a breath and began again, piling up the last of the carrots, at least until the next morning's delivery. "You think old Hugo can keep everything the same no matter how you behave. That's not how it works, not when you go traveling around unannounced. Think about it. No one wants to see you on Seventh East without your harmonica."

He heard a motor start, glanced out the door, and placed the shovel in the tool corner. He latched the elephant-proof gates to protect the larder and tool cupboard. Princess Alice likely would find her own uses for a broom, shovel, and even the bull hook if she had the chance. With a sigh, he bent and unlocked the chain on Princess's massive back ankle so she could reach her fruit and amble over to her favorite sleeping corner under the heavily screened window. A cursory pat on her trunk, and he swung the barn door closed, double-locked it, and checked all the locks around the building.

The Ferris wheel tune, garbled with the carousel chimes, grew fainter as he ambled wearily across the lawn toward his home on lower Harvard Avenue. Sometimes he wondered if he was the reason Princess Alice seemed to favor Seventh East for her jaunts. Did she know he lived in that direction?

Hell, some morning I'll wake up to find the princess helping Anna in the kitchen, he thought.

He couldn't get too frustrated with the old girl. She was

smarter than any person, including himself, he knew. She wanted a change of scenery once in a while, and she really should be encouraged to have another calf to focus her energies, but the politics, logistics, and dangers of bringing a bull in *musth* made Hugo shudder. Besides, Princess Alice had mourned loudly and long when Prince Utah had died shortly before his first birthday.

That had been a royal mess! One night the calf had curled up in a blind spot behind Princess, who had inadvertently rolled over on him in her sleep. From across the park the next morning, Hugo heard Princess's heartbroken wails, and he had hastened to the enclosure. He found her trying to lift the injured calf, which bleated pitifully but could not stand and would not nurse. After he died, Princess guarded the body for hours, spurting a stream of tears and wailing. Sometimes Hugo thought he still heard sorrow as an undertone in her rumbles and sighs.

Prince Utah's death also meant a financial loss to the city, as well as keen disappointment for zoo visitors, so it was a sad occasion all around. Hugo had heard that some enterprising taxidermist was stuffing the calf for display at the new zoo, which he considered to be a paramount reason to keep Princess Alice away. She would smell her calf even if she never saw his preserved image.

Would Americans want their dead child on display next door? he wondered.

Well, perhaps they would, if it was a good likeness. Americans were strange when it came to dressing up bodies. Where Hugo came from, families washed and dressed their dead, but no one coiffed their hair or applied wax or cosmetics so they would appear rosy-cheeked in their caskets.

His current goal was to keep the elephant healthy and just

stimulated enough so that boredom would not lead her into trouble. New tricks not only complemented her repertoire but kept her alert and happy. Besides, soon the moon would be full and they would have a midnight adventure. At least Princess wasn't getting beaten by a circus trainer or being shot at by ivory hunters and bush-meat poachers.

He walked a little faster, whistling "Bicycle Built for Two," whimsically picturing Princess pedaling the bike. The truth was, he had the best job in the world and the shortest commute, with his home a few blocks from the park—that is, when Princess Alice didn't ruin the situation by behaving like a wild animal.

⚷

Sol woke early, did his watering, and then relaxed on his screened porch, eating dry Rice Krispies with his fingers. He had found an extension cord in the basement. Pleased, he brought his radio out onto the porch so he could hear the interruptions in the programing for bulletins to be alert for a missing four-year-old boy. Four was really too young an age for a child to be interesting, he had decided. Probably the youngest child he had ever known well was Junie, and she had been about six.

He contemplated the little girl who lived next door in a rental unit when Sol was about thirteen. She had collected marbles and would trade nearly anything for a cat's-eye. Resourcefully, Sol had rescued a whole bag of marbles from a closet shelf, some long-ago Christmas gift from an uncle, and when he displayed the bag, Junie became his fast friend. Slowly he learned that girls love to pretend. Even playing house could have its rewards.

The one thing Sol knew best about himself was that he was lazy. He had tried babysitting, but it was too much work. To his surprise, parents expected him to prepare meals and wash the dishes. Plus, brothers and sisters got in the way of his friendship with a coveted child. Besides that, a babysitter was the first one anyone suspected if something went wrong. He had been to jail and had not liked it.

Anyway, he did not have to babysit or be tall and handsome. He didn't even have to hunt girlfriends because they would come to him.

As if on cue, the murmur and rhythmic steps of hopscotch ruffled his reverie. He adjusted his cotton trousers and peered out a side screen. As he suspected, Mary Agnes had redrawn her hopscotch on the front sidewalk even though she lived several blocks east. She tossed her hoppie taw into square 2.

"Hey!" he barked. "Don't you know it's illegal to block the sidewalk?"

She whirled toward him, pale with embarrassment, and then cross. "Shut up, you stupid! You'll ruin my whole game."

"Sor-ry," he wheedled. "How about a popsicle when you finish?"

She kept hopping. "I'm not supposed to talk to grown-ups," she said. "Not even big kids like you."

"Oh, smart idea. I know. I'll pull up my chair so I can see you step on the lines. If you don't, well then you can come up here and I'll find you a popsicle."

Mary Agnes shrugged and kept her gaze peeled to the sidewalk. He felt a second's unease. Was Mary Agnes, so skinny with her thin mousy hair, jumbled teeth, and wrinkly play clothes, really worth his trouble? For today, maybe, at least for information. He put four fingers in his mouth and gave her a wolf whistle as she tossed for 4. He noticed a slight smile on her face.

Awkwardly, triumphantly, she at last jumped her final round through the chalk lines. Sol stood and applauded. "Looks like I'd better go find that popsicle," he crowed.

She tossed a dubious look back over her shoulder, almost flirty, he thought. "Better come up on the porch. It's cooler so it won't melt so fast."

Sol went hastily inside, thinking she might follow, but no; when he returned, he found her in his chair. "So I get to sit on *your* lap," he said.

She hopped up so fast, he worried he had warned her off, but she still reached for the popsicle. She winked her dark eyes, alternating one and then the other like a railroad crossing sign. "Bet you can't wink both eyes like I can."

"True," he said. He sat down and licked his own treat.

She giggled. "You really can't do it?"

He winked back just once. "Ma-ry Ag-nes," he crooned, once her lips and chin turned lurid with red syrup. "Look how pretty you are with your lips stained red. Say, do you happen to know those girls who go to the park a lot? They look like they're about your age."

"What girls?" She gazed across the street as if expecting to see them materialize.

"They live back that way, I think. South of me. Two of them look alike, maybe sisters. They have these long braids. The other one, their friend, is a blondie."

Mary Agnes nodded and licked faster, but cherry-flavored juice dribbled down her neck into the top of her faded sunsuit. Sol went inside for a wash rag. She crinkled her nose at its sour smell but took it to clean herself up. "Is it okay if I keep the popsicle stick?"

"Sure is," he said. "You can have mine, too. Now come

here and tell me who those girls are. They aren't half as friendly as you."

"Stuck up," Mary Agnes nodded, sliding into the chair beside him. "Those two with the braids? Well, they are just about famous at school for being identical twins." She screwed up her face. "But really, they *aren't* twins at all because there are three of them. Triples, is that what you call them?"

"Triplets," Sol corrected. "They're triplets."

Mary Agnes heard the wonder in his voice and turned away. "Well, so what?" she said. "I'm glad I'm not a triple or have a cop in my house." She stood, clearly prepared to leave.

"Wait," Sol said, "do you want another popsicle?—or a cookie?"

She shook her head.

"What cop?"

But Mary Agnes had returned to her hopscotch and refused to acknowledge his entreaties. Maybe she was jealous. Or she recalled her mother's warning about a missing child, although the folks across Seventh East probably wouldn't be too apprehensive. Maybe he shouldn't have slid a finger under the hem of her shorts.

Triplets and a cop in the house? Now that was rather interesting.

four

With Evan working, Rose Flynn decided to clean up after dinner alone, sending Glenn off to work at the gas station, Joyce over to her friend Peggy's house, and the triplets out to play. The children's chores were designed more to teach them than to spare her work. The house needed a discerning eye and she needed time to herself, though she'd rather wash dishes when Evan was there to dry them.

She smiled as she loaded the sink. To think how long it had taken her and her sister Beryl, as children, to concede that husbands were necessary, at least to justify placing baby dolls under their overalls to await birth. Even living on a farm, their mother had managed to keep them from connecting scraps of information they picked up from random observations. They heard about fertile hens and stud bulls without comprehending any real meaning to it. How much simpler to dispatch imaginary husbands off to work and overseas on church missions, organizing their dolls around a mother's domestic chores, rather than including men.

Rose did not miss the farm. She had gathered eggs with her sisters and driven the combine for her brothers without any particular wish to continue. Most of her siblings had scattered except for Beryl, who married a train engineer and lived in Ogden, north of Salt Lake, and Shirley, still single, who taught elementary school and lived with their parents as they sold acres of farmland.

In her own home, Rose found every task layered with memories. She and Evan had purchased the bungalow, their first house, in 1922, the year Joyce was born. By then, Glennie was becoming too aware to park his crib at the end of their bed. With a second baby, they needed a real nursery.

On Evan's first day off after being promoted to the Theft & Burglary Department, they had begun house hunting, attracted to the new neighborhoods near Liberty Park. While still on patrol, Evan had responded to a call regarding a naked woman in an orchard behind a white frame house on Lake Street, south of Seventeenth South. He found a local artist of some renown there, James T. Harwood, armed with a beret, easel, and oils. The man was painting his naked wife as she posed on a broad bench, and this was the celebrated artist who had a painting hanging in the City and County Building!

"Carpenters were banging a kitchen nook onto one side of the house," he told Rose, "and kids were racing around; but there she was, absolutely motionless and wearing nothing." He concluded he thought they wanted "a brick house closer in to town, in a neighborhood where people still wear clothes."

"Agreed," she responded.

The five-year-old bungalow they eventually chose featured deep red bricks with sparkling white trim and dormers. From the start, Rose had liked the graceful arch between the parlor and dining room and the inconspicuous door leading from the dining room to their bedroom, which was cool and dark as a cave with pear-tinted light filtering through the pulled blind. The bathroom, its porcelain fixtures gleaming, opened onto their bedroom and kitchen. The latter already held a table and some unmatched wooden chairs, as if to show where to spread the rug under the dining set they would buy, away from meal-time messes the babies would make in the kitchen.

She laughed thinking how spacious the house had seemed for her little family—like the song she hummed to her off-spring at bedtime:

We shall raise a fa-mi-ly:
A boy for you, a girl for me.
Can't you see how happy
We will be-e-e.

Then, five years later, chaos! The kitchen arrangement, for instance, lasted only until the triplets learned to sit up. They had to move meals into the dining room after all, spreading a plastic sheet under the high chairs.

They bundled the triplets sideways in a single crib for a while. Evan's fellow officers helped him frame an attic room for Glenn, then almost eight, and for Joycie, who was five. They obtained two more cribs from a secondhand store and put them in the back bedroom, using the adjoining room for baby equipment and toys. Evan completed the renovations before he was shot during a bank robbery, which reduced his helpfulness for a while.

They had been so unprepared back then! Rose had sus-pected when she was seven months gone that she might be carrying twins, but the doctor had said it would be another big fine boy. No one had suspected tiny triplets, barely five pounds each, born premature and more demanding than either of their siblings had been. They needed lots of care.

They could not turn to Evan's family. His brothers still lived in Philadelphia, where their parents had died of influenza. Rose's family helped out by hiring an extra summer hand for the farm and allowing Shirley, who was in high school, to bicycle over each morning. For the first two weeks, Evan took vacation leave, and between the three of them they were able to organize the rounds of changing, feeding, and endless laundry and preparation of sterilized bottles.

Glenn proved surprisingly eager too. He fed, rocked, and burped his infant sisters, in exchange for an occasional lift across Ninth East to play with his best buddy, Archie, away from Joyce and her next-door-neighbor friend Peggy and their annoying girlish games.

Rose reminisced as she wiped the counter and stove, secretly still feeling that something irreplaceable had broken inside her. She could not imagine racing Glenn from the yard through the alley and back around like she used to do or whirling Joyce until they both felt dizzy. Evan seemed to accept her lessened energy level as he met his own demands of work and helped with the babies while recuperating from his bullet wound.

For one thing, Rose mused as she swept, the babies were mostly interested in each other. They reached their tiny hands out to connect with each other and curled up together as if they were still packed within their mother's womb. Yet each was distinct from the beginning, especially to Rose. Bethany, of course, stood out with her fair hair, but she also developed an intent gaze and a habit of clasping her tiny hands before her. Annabel and Carolee were both dark, but Annabel's hair topped a head that tended to redden, and she startled the easiest and cried the loudest, always with her spine arched. Carolee's flourishes and kicks appeared purposeful, as if she already intended to direct the events around her.

They were born at the end of May and had to be kept indoors for a month. Finally in July they were taken to church to blessed and officially named. This gave Rose and her sister, Beryl, time to make blessing dresses. Even as babies, Rose hadn't wanted them to be dressed alike; her daughters might be a packaged set to the world, but not to her. Beryl found the right fabric for the three little dresses in complementary pale blue, faint green, and fairy lavender, as well as the lining and embroidery thread in slightly darker shades. Together the sisters had created simple but elegant tiny dresses with little puffed sleeves, abbreviated yokes, and gathered skirts. In odd bits of time, Rose embroidered the borders above the hems with a delicate wildflower and butterfly motif and adorned six satin shoes to match. The tiny shoes soon went into Rose's cedar chest, but the dresses proved more practical as sweet, washable outfits for special occasions.

Over the summer, Rose felt her strength return, but the wild joy that had spun her into an occasional delirium of play or lust was gone. On July 17, when the triplets were only six weeks old, Rose received the telephone call that every police officer's wife dreads.

"I'm all right, Rosebud," Evan had said in a voice that squeaked a bit, "but now it's my turn to go to the hospital. Some knucklehead shot at me while he was dashing down the sidewalk. He managed to hit my arm."

A nurse had taken the telephone to explain the good news that although the bullet had fractured two bones before passing through the left forearm, "the doctor believes he can set it without surgery. If all goes well, your husband should be sleeping at home tonight," she had said cheerfully.

Initially Rose felt only profound relief that Evan had not been killed or more seriously wounded. He probably wouldn't be admitted as a patient, so she shouldn't bother coming to the hospital, he had urged. Once she hung up, though, she wondered how she could have even considered going to the hospital with five children under the age of eight to look after. Even when Evan was back, she calculated, they would have only one functioning arm per triplet.

Late that afternoon when his partner deposited him at home, Evan was ashen, shaky, and encased in plaster from shoulder to fingertip. By then, Rose had regained her composure. She cradled Carolee in one arm as she helped settle Evan onto the sofa. Glenn and Joyce each rocked a baby beside the radio, and Rose's younger sister, Shirley, fixed supper. Rose had not wanted Beryl to make another long trip from Ogden, especially when she had already done so much.

"Keep your arm up on the pillows even if you doze off," Rose reminded Evan.

That night when Evan moved to their bed, he kept his left arm propped up and crowned it with ice. The pain pill didn't seem to dull the pain but at least made him feel woozy. Rose edged down carefully onto the bed on his other side until, predictably at about midnight, Annabel began to fuss. Before Rose had been able to remove the baby's gauze diaper, Bethany had begun crying, then Carolee began to whimper.

Who should come to the rescue but Glenn, tucking a warmed bottle under his chin and carefully lifting Annabel. Rose settled Bethany and reached for Carolee. "I woke Aunt Shirley as soon as I got downstairs," Glenn said. "She'll be right in."

Rose thanked him. "Let's see if we can let Joycie sleep
through the night since she's still so young."

Glenn offered his mother a grave, appraising look which
belied his years. "No kidding, Mom. Otherwise she'll be a
screaming meanie all day tomorrow."

In early September when Glenn turned eight, he wasn't
baptized until his father's cast came off since Evan had to be able
to dip his son backward into the font. The family gathered downtown at the turtle-backed Tabernacle to see Glenn immersed in
the water, Evan demonstrating the requisite strength.

Rose recalled how on weekdays, she had tucked three tiny
babies into one well-used buggy to walk Joyce and Glenn south
to Hawthorne Elementary School. Usually Evan's schedule
proved flexible enough to pick up Joyce after her kindergarten
session and take her home. Displaced from her role as baby of
the family, and with the additional adjustment of school, the
five-year-old enjoyed the uninterrupted time with her father
without her brother or the triplets around. Rose also tried to sit
down with Joyce sometimes for lunch or read a story together
while the triplets napped.

When the weather turned cold, Evan arranged for his
partner to drive so Rose could have the car for running errands.
She would bundle the babies into an oversized car bed and
stow the folded buggy into the trunk and make do as best she
could. Once the girls turned three and could safely navigate
stairs, the children switched bedrooms again, Evan turning the
two small bedrooms upstairs into one large room for the triplets and Glenn and Joyce moving back downstairs. Now that
the two oldest were teenagers, they forbade their mother from
entering their rooms without invitation.

Deciding that she might as well track down towels for the

day's wash, Rose glanced into Joyce's messy little haven, and the first thing she noticed was a cream petticoat draped over the bedpost. She was going to ask Joyce—who was straightening her closet again—but changed her mind. *I do work in Lingerie, and it was on sale, plus my employee discount*, is what Joyce would no doubt say. Sixteen was not the easiest age. Rose and Evan found their daughter's queenly airs amusing. For his part, Glenn had become quietly evasive, although he remained Evan's assistant when it came to repairs and heavy lifting.

Rose began tossing items into wicker bins. Years back Evan had enclosed the back porch for her washing machine and electric wringer to be near the rows of clotheslines in the backyard, bordered by lilac bushes that lined the fences. Rose learned how to modestly conceal their temple garments by hanging them on the inner lines and putting the white sheets on the outer ones. Lacking a garage, the yard had a tool shed and parking area between the lawn and alley. In the basement a plywood partition kept shelves of bottled fruit and vegetables separate from Evan's tabletop drill and other tools. Over the years, he had tried to interest Glenn in various woodworking projects, but Glenn preferred tinkering with anything on wheels.

Then Glenn began dating Margie, a pretty girl who was a year ahead of Joyce at South High School. Rose didn't know how they would manage the car when Joyce became a junior and learned to drive. Things would be even more hectic when the little girls became teens. She decided not to think about it right now and to read for a bit before calling in the triplets.

x—⊤

Joyce sat on the floor of her lighted closet, its open door shielding her from her mother's view. Her closet was too small, and her slim chest of drawers held only her lingerie, including her stockings. Even doubling her blouses and skirts on the same hangers, and her trousers with her jackets, she had insufficient closet space for her growing wardrobe. She figured that when the time came to buy school clothes for the new year and Papa augmented her own earnings, she would be well-outfitted, if she could just find a place for everything.

Recently she had befriended Sybil, a manager in the third-floor Ladies Wear department, who had made it easy to try on clothes during breaks or before work. Sometimes Sybil kept an eye on the floor from just outside the dressing rooms while they chatted, but even then she rarely noticed *exactly* what Joyce had carried into the dressing room and what she carried out. Besides, with wages so low, Joyce assumed everyone on the staff slipped away an unpurchased item now and again anyway.

Joyce had greater finesse at getting purloined merchandise out the door than Wanda, who sadly got fired. The best technique was to take advantage of the spacious customer restroom for final adjustments. It didn't do to leave the building with an extra layer that appeared bulky. Joyce didn't have a guilty face to betray her either; she had overcome that back when she was five and began slipping a roll of Life Savers into her pocket from the rack at the market. She hid the candy beneath the lilac bush nearest the alley and treated herself to one when the babies' *Now! Now! Now!* screams for bottles made her frantic.

Joyce had been the little girl on Papa's knee, the sweetheart in Mama's lap, until Mama's lap disappeared under a twitching bulge; suddenly Joyce became the big sister instead. Oh, her parents praised her occasional help, and she liked the babies better once they ceased resembling frantic red chickens, yet the stolen candy continued to ease her nerves and remained her secret therapy as she grew older.

She was, after all, a cop's daughter. She knew from her father's suppertime tales of crime that thieves got caught because they were stupid and careless. Well, she was neither— so skilled that she would never get caught.

With no progress on the Frankie Stuart case, police scrutiny returned to burglars and parole violators. Lieutenants and captains began cutting back on their officers' overtime hours. Unless a lead came in, it was time to give everyone a break and save the city money.

Evan was glad to be reliably home in the evenings again. Tonight, he gathered his family together after dinner to discuss a crisis before Glenn left for the gas station. Bobby, the two-year-old from next door, had joined them for dinner and now settled into Rose's lap. Evan noticed that the Terrible Trio went cross-eyed in unison when they sat down and faced their older siblings across the table. Glenn just grinned at them. Even Joyce, for once, didn't rise to the bait.

"All right, everyone," Evan began, "we have a bit of a family emergency. You all know that your Aunt Shirley contracted a bad case of the mumps." Around the table heads nodded.

"Aunt Shirley?" Bobby wondered.

"Yes. Well, now she's showing early signs of whooping cough. Doc Sanders says she needs more nursing care than your grandmother can provide her. On top of that, Grandma never had whooping cough. We don't want her catching it now."

Joyce's throat tightened. She could see what was coming as clearly as a tornado taking shape in Kansas. *They'll want me to quit my summer job and nurse Aunt Shirley at the farm!* she panicked. Her mind escaped to picture the tall sinuous frame of Harvey Pratt in Men's Wear. Just the thought of him created the same startling flame that flared inside her every time he sauntered past her counter. Yesterday he had winked. Before long he was going to ask her to the movies or to lunch in the Tiffin Room. So far, he hadn't, and he *never* would if she disappeared now.

"Don't ask me to quit my job," she pleaded. "The discount will save you money on school clothes."

"Now, you're jumping way ahead of me, sister. We need you to help, but not on the farm. For one thing, all of us have had pertussis."

"But I haven't had the mumps," Glenn put in.

"Have I had the mumps?" Bobby asked.

Rose shook her head. "I don't think so, and you might as well while you're little."

Evan flashed an impatient frown to the other end of the table. Interpreting it correctly, Rose scooped up Bobby and took him home. When she returned to the table, Evan was still reasoning with their own children, saying, "You sure as blazes don't want to get the mumps now, son."

Bethany exchanged looks with Carolee to her left and Annabel on her right. "Why shouldn't Glenn just get the mumps, too?" she asked logically. "Then he won't have to worry about it later."

Her mother shook her head slightly, but Evan shrugged.

"Because if he catches mumps now he might not have children. With older boys, mumps have a tendency to fall."

To *fall?* This sounded like a baseball game with all the catching and falling. Carolee began to ask more, but her father waved her off.

"The point is that our family has been really lucky during these hard years. Sometimes downtown I see kids so skinny you wouldn't believe it. We find whole families sick with hookworm and measles. Well, now it's our turn to show we can pull together. After supper, Glenn, pack a bag and take it to work. We already checked with Archie's mother and you can go home from the gas station with him and stay there for a few days. Hopefully Shirley is almost over the mumps part, and when we're sure the contagion is gone, you can move back home.

"I'm counting on you four girls to help your mother turn this dining room into a sickroom right after dinner," he said, reaching for Joyce's hand to give it a squeeze. He knew she would hate what came next. "Before work, Glenn, I will take apart and store the dining room table and then break down Joyce's full-size bed and bring it in here for Shirley. Joyce, you can sleep with Mama. And the five of you ought to fit around the kitchen table all right."

Five?

Evan noted his children exchange looks, but he hadn't reached that part yet.

"Aunt Beryl will drive Aunt Shirley over here tonight. Then she and her kids will scrub down the farmhouse in hopes that Grandma and Grandpa can stay healthy. Okay, everyone clear on that?"

His family nodded, although Bethany and Carolee obviously brimmed with questions. Annabel echoed Joyce's sigh. Both of them hated to see their routines broken up. Annabel found a strand of comfort. *At least I get to sleep in my own bed upstairs.*

"Okay, now here's the hardest part," Evan continued. "I'm going to be bunking at the police station because Doctor Sanders is going to slap big yellow-and-black quarantine signs on our door. Nobody will be able to go past the front porch or beyond the clotheslines in back. Once Aunt Shirley is here, don't play with anyone outside. Nobody but the doc or a public health nurse can come inside.

"I know it will be hard but I'm counting on every one of you." He looked at Bethany. "Please respect the quarantine and don't sneak away, even to see Princess Alice. You'd risk making everyone you see sick, and maybe Princess too." Evan had no idea actually if elephants could catch either mumps or whooping cough, and he ordinarily didn't lie to his children, but he knew the threat of making the elephant ill might keep Bethany away from her. "Joyce, I'll talk with your supervisor at work. I'd let you stay with a friend like your brother is going to, but your mother will need you. The Terrible Trio will help, too, but you're more capable. Hopefully this won't last too long and the ZCMI won't hire someone else in your place."

Joyce swallowed back tears. *Does Papa have any idea what he's saying? Does he know how many girls want my summer job?* "Glenn would be better to do this, Papa. Remember how good he was with the babies?"

Glenn blushed. He said nothing but his brain excitedly traced the short distance between the homes of his friend Archie and his steady girlfriend, Margie. *No curfew!* he thought.

"Think of your aunt," Evan replied. "Wouldn't she be more comfortable with a niece caring for her than her nineteen-year-old nephew?"

Joyce began to protest that the doctor, after all, was male, but looked at her mother's worried face and the triplets about to explode with the drama of it all. She considered what would happen if someone decided to scrutinize her overloaded closet while she was away. She reached deep for resolve.

"Please call Lois for me, Papa," she said. "She works in the evenings. Don't worry, you can count on me to help out."

"I know I can," he replied. "I'm counting on each of you. Please be kind through this and help your mother and," his eyes traveled over the trio and then lit on Glenn, "don't take advantage of the situation. Maybe once things calm down, we can arrange some kind of family outing as a reward."

"We can visit the Dionnes in Canada," Carolee whispered and clasped her hands.

"I was thinking more along the lines of the new zoo," her father said drily and pushed back his chair. "Let's get the furniture moved, Glenn, and then pack. I don't want you late for your shift."

⚷

Evan called Lois Wheeler, Joyce's supervisor, from the station. His explanation was met by a rather long silence.

"We really can't hold positions for part-time workers," she said. "But I do understand. I suppose my first concern is that Joyce can sign her time sheets for the last two weeks."

"I'm downtown. Maybe I can swing by and pick those up for her. How late do you expect to be there?"

"Another hour or so," Lois said. "However, I expected Joyce to work tomorrow and then record her time. I won't be in on Saturday, but I suppose I can ask the Notions staff to cover our department."

"Sounds fine, but Joyce will be quarantined by tomorrow, so let's get those time sheets taken care of tonight."

He parked outside the store and found his daughter's supervisor in Lingerie. "I don't suppose I could just sign these for her?" he asked while leaning on the counter to compensate for Lois's petite size. She had dark hair and a bright smile, he noted with a policeman's eye for detail and a man's eye for a nice-looking woman. She seemed to be about thirty or so and wore no rings on her small hands.

"I'm sorry to put you to so much trouble, but I wouldn't want to encourage you to commit forgery. You'd have to arrest yourself," she added with a grin.

"Well then, it looks like a quick trip home. I'll be right back. Say," he added impulsively, "why don't you ride with me and explain this to Joyce?"

She paused for a moment, perhaps not wanting to promise anything about guaranteed employment, perhaps not wishing to accompany a stranger. Then she agreed. As they drove, he had the station patch him through to his home telephone and asked Joyce to watch for their arrival.

With the car windows lowered to enjoy the cooling air, he and Lois made the usual small talk about work. She had begun at ZCMI as a high school part-timer like Joyce, then took a full-time position after she graduated from LDS Business College. However, she was interested in his rise through the ranks as a police officer.

"How long does it take to become a lieutenant?" she asked.

"Longer than I've been there," he explained. It was all right that he hadn't advanced that far, he said, because he was "not ready yet to get stuck behind a desk. I already spend too much time there," he added.

As they passed the park, Lois laughed to hear Princess Alice trumpeting. "Visiting Princess Alice used to be my favorite thing to do on my birthday. I loved ice skating on Liberty Lake too. My fingers and toes would freeze off before I was ready to quit."

Another blast, fainter this time. "It sounds like Princess is in her barn," Evan said. "I met her trainer recently. When she comes out to greet the public, the sound is twice as loud."

Watching from the car as Lois and Joyce consulted on the front porch, Evan suspected that he had helped preserve his daughter's summer job. Considering their worry over Shirley, he felt remarkably lighthearted. He wanted to suggest stopping at Hires Root Beer Drive-in during the fifteen-minute trip back downtown, but that would seem wrong for a married man to do. He assumed Lois was single. Instead, they made the trip almost in silence except for the constant, static-filled chatter on the dispatch radio.

"Thanks for going out of your way," she said as he pulled up to the curb. "I hope Joyce can return to us soon."

"Likewise. I'll give you a wave next time I'm in the store."

Another bright smile, and she was on her way toward the employee entrance. He admired the swing of her navy skirt and her practical choice of flat shoes. So many petite women staggered around on high heels.

"Lead me not into temptation," he muttered to himself. "My life is complicated enough."

As he pulled into traffic, the dispatcher reported an alleged Frankie Stuart sighting. Apparently Evan would be working tonight after all. "Ten-four," he responded. "I'm on my way."

By midnight, Rose's sewing machine and all the fabric and

patterns that could not fit into the oak buffet had been hauled down to the basement. They placed Joyce's bed where the table had been, and alongside the bed they placed the telephone table from the front hall, covered with a vinyl tablecloth folded to fit. Annabel found the family's enamel basins under the bathroom sink and stacked them next to a pile of old towels and wash cloths.

Shirley collapsed into bed when she arrived about midnight. She had become unrecognizable, her flushed and swollen face flaming like the sun setting through the clouds. She whimpered like a toddler through her swollen jaw. She was unable to unlatch her molars. More than anything, she needed to hold onto someone's hand—anyone's hand. The only medicines that might help her were aspirin and cough syrup. Evan had made sure they had plenty of both. Soon the tin pitcher and sections of old towels filled the space and the smell of sickness began to fill the house.

Rose tucked her in, but Shirley was in too much pain to rest. For hours, Rose and Joyce alternated the application of hot towels and ice bags against her jaws, but Shirley coughed so hard the towels dropped off and tears flooded her lumpy cheeks. Blowing her stuffy nose brought another layer of pain. By dawn her whooping woke the triplets upstairs.

Carolee headed the second string of attendants so her mother and Joyce could catch a few hours of sleep, although Rose insisted that the door between the dining room and master bedroom stay open so she could hear if anything went wrong. Shirley coughed up quantities of a vile yellow gunk that smelled awful. Annabel rinsed basin after basin without complaint. Bethany piled soiled cloths into a washtub of hot water to which she added Borax.

Rose was so relieved to have her children's help, she collapsed into an overstuffed chair and dozed off. Soon Shirley fell asleep as well, so Joyce stretched out, fully dressed, on her mother's unmade bed to nap. The triplets gazed out the front window, watching for the doctor. There were nearly twenty minutes of peace before Shirley started coughing and whooping, and it all began again.

⚷

Throughout his shift at the gas station, Glenn did not know or care whether his father experienced temptation. In Glenn's view, his father was married and could have sex anytime, though the actual idea of his parents having sex was not something he dwelled on. What mattered to Glenn was that tonight he had no curfew. Too bad he didn't have a car either. In fact, he had taken the job at the gas station in the hope that one day someone would bring in a jalopy for repairs and let it go cheap, but he'd had no luck there.

At nine he locked the station and left with Archie. He knew from Boy Scout trips that his friend usually fell asleep quickly and soundly. He also knew from dates and phone calls that Margie liked to stay up late. *Perfect!* Their houses were only two blocks apart. With no parent watching over his shoulder, tonight felt like fate.

Dating Margie had proven to be a thrilling but frustrating adventure. The boys agreed that she was a cutie, with long arms and legs and enticing curves. Not only did a curfew thwart his attempts to see her at night, so did his father's reluctance to let him take the family car. Margie was welcome at the Flynn home to make fudge or dance to records as long as his parents were home.

Which stunk. *Doesn't Pop know what trouble the triplets are?* he wondered. *So is Joyce, come to think of it.* Whenever Margie came by, Joyce liked to chat with her about everything from clothes to high school, not realizing that this was supposed to be a date and that the two might want some time alone! He wasn't comfortable at Margie's house, though, where he wasn't especially welcome, so they fell into the habit of riding the bus downtown and window shopping or walking through Liberty Park.

He liked to steal kisses on the ferris wheel and on the paddle boats. The trees in the park cast welcome shadows too, but that didn't compare to the privacy that must be possible in a Hudson parked on the side of a county road. *Pop must know that!* Just as Margie started to become more affectionate and willing, his father had made their search for privacy increasingly impossible.

He wondered if Pop's caution had anything to do with Mrs. Landers, whose boyfriend dropped by and stayed long enough to create whispers at church. Glenn couldn't remember the man's name; Margie referred to her mother's boyfriend only as *the creep.* Truth be told, Glenn didn't like Darlene either because she seemed so coarse and brusque. That didn't matter now.

No curfew tonight!

He threw his bedroll onto Archie's bedroom floor, borrowed a pillow, and pretended to be drowsy. As anticipated, Archie was sleeping by ten o'clock. Glenn grabbed his bedroll and unlatched the back screen door, then slipped outside into a chorus of crickets whose music accompanied his stride to Margie's house. Cautiously heading around back, he found her light still on, and she immediately appeared when he tapped on the glass. She slid easily out the window into his arms, her shiny hair messy, her arms and legs bare. She laughed softly when she saw that he had brought his bedroll.

"I thought we could look at the stars."

"Isn't it kind of cloudy?" She laughed again. "Silly you."

"Well, and maybe kiss a little."

"Just a little?"

He changed the subject. "What do you call this outfit?"

"Shorty pajamas. Doesn't Joyce have some?"

"Who knows?" He didn't want to think about his sister. Clearly Margie was far more mature. She was going to be a senior in the fall.

"Come back this way," she whispered, and led him to the darkest corner of the yard. The thickness of the bedroll made up for the sparse grass.

They had dated for over a year, and tonight her silken skin plus his own urgency quickly overcame him. They kissed and touched so long that clothes seemed unnecessary and even absurd, to which Margie evidently agreed! The sensation of her body against his dazzled him. Instinctively, he pushed against her as she wound her arms and legs around him. Then with a gasp, he realized the amazing fact contained in adult innuendo and kids' jokes. *Incredible!* He had imagined this to be far more difficult; her heat and his pressure combined to end the bliss all too soon.

When he caught his breath, he rolled up on an elbow to suggest they start over again. *Why not?* But Margie was reaching for her clothes, avoiding his eyes, sponging between her legs with her underwear.

"Margie! What—?"

Her instincts proved right. No sooner had she pulled on her pajama top than the light went on over the back porch. "Mar-gie?" He began struggling to put on his own clothes.

68

"I'm coming, Darlene." She took a long step away from Glenn toward the light. "It's such a pretty night, I just wanted to look at the stars."

"It's going to rain any minute now! I don't want you out there alone." Her mother vanished into the house.

"Wait!" He stumbled forward and caught Margie's hand. "Just—just wait. Come back."

"I can't. Creep is gone."

"Not even a kiss good night?"

"Haven't you had enough?" Her voice sounded tense—guilty? But it had been so wonderful! He watched her walk over to the metal garbage can, drop her underwear into it, and quietly replace the lid before sliding through the back door.

In a mad swirl of yearning and gratitude, he folded the bedroll and walked back to Archie's bungalow. As he did so, he tried to replay every kiss, every caress. *So amazing.*

So extraordinary! We have to do it again. Is Margie mad at me? Did I hurt her?

He didn't think so. She had been fine until they were interrupted. If only she had waited for a last embrace, at least a quick kiss. Maybe she feared him getting carried away again. That was it—she just feared getting caught.

Next time, now that he understood the process, he promised himself to go more slowly, to get her to talk, find out what she liked most. *Next time*, the crickets sang in the long grass, *next time, next time, next time* … As he replayed the event in his mind, he decided in the future, when he removed her clothes, he should tell her how beautiful she was and that he loved her. Well, he did love her, didn't he? That's what he would do next time.

How many nights were there before he would have to move back home, he wondered? He resolved to enjoy his freedom while he could. Really, he should move away from home. Wasn't that more important than buying a set of wheels? All the well-paying jobs went to older men who had families. Maybe he could grab an extra shift once in a while, save for a basement apartment, even a room somewhere.

He knew his mother had long hoped he would fill a church mission. But who could afford to go on a mission these days? Besides, he hated talking to strangers even to say *Fill 'er up?* or *Here's your change*. A studio apartment sounded more like heaven right now than anything he had ever heard about at church.

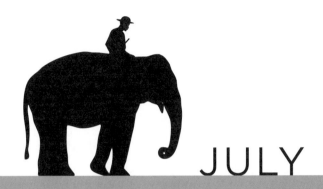

JULY

six

Doc Sanders shook his tousled gray head when Rose begged for something more for Shirley, even a medicine that hadn't been fully tested yet. "I'm sorry," he said. "You're doing all that can be done. Even in the hospital on State Street, they couldn't do more."

He took Rose's hand and added, "Actually, you should be glad Shirley isn't hospitalized. Right now the second and third floors seem like one big charity ward, full of contagious diseases and the nasty things that go with poverty. Chances are, she would pick up something else in the hospital."

"I *am* glad she's not there and I appreciate your help. I just wish there was something else we could try."

"Just try to make her comfortable and keep giving her clear fluids."

The doctor glanced at Carolee, who was listening at her mother's elbow, then shot Rose a keen look from under his grizzled eyebrows. "Rose, I guess you've already given your sister a blessing?"

"My father and the bishop gave her a blessing before we

moved her. Of course, we can't get anyone else in here with the quarantine."

"No need, since it's already been done," he said. He packed his bag and jotted a rough schedule of his daily rounds in case they needed to reach him and set it on the buffet. "Call me if you need to."

He paused to tickle Bethany under the chin. "I remember delivering you," he said. "I told your mother you and your sisters were going to be a triple threat, and here you are." Turning back to Rose, he added, "Don't wear yourself out, now. You tend to Shirley for three hours, then rest while Joyce takes the next three hours. Rotate the triplets as your assistants. Remember that this won't go on forever."

They tried the shifts, the same as they tried all the doctor's suggestions. One afternoon Joyce stumbled into the bedroom and stretched out on the bed next to her mother. For a minute or two, mother and daughter gave into exhaustion and lay side by side. Then they looked at one another, alarmed.

"Something's changed," Rose said, pushing herself up by her elbows.

They listened. "It's *quiet*," Joyce said. "Maybe she's stopped whooping."

They rushed into the next room to find Shirley staring glassily at the ceiling while Bethany read to her. Rose shook down the thermometer, slid it under Shirley's tongue, and took up Shirley's wrist, then dropped it reflexively. "She's on fire!"

The thermometer showed a fever of over 104 degrees. Prompted by her mother, Joyce anxiously searched through the toweling and slips of scratch paper to find the doctor's schedule. When she reached him by telephone, he was north of the park. He asked Joyce to put her mother on the phone.

"Pneumonia," he told her after she reported the fever and soft, thick cough that had just begun. "It's a common complication, considering how long she's been sick. I'll bring by some sulfa, but it might be too late. Use more ice. Wrap it up and tuck it under her arms along her sides. You need to try to bring her fever down, Rose. But remember, I don't need any more patients."

While Joyce emptied the ice cube trays, Rose called Evan at the police station. "Please get us more ice," she said, after filling him in. "Just leave whatever you can find at the bottom of the porch steps."

"Will do. I wish I could do more to help."

As they waited for Evan to arrive, Rose gathered her daughters at Shirley's bedside for a family prayer. By the time they had heated soup and taken turns eating, the ice arrived, and they packed it in towels around Shirley's torso and behind her neck. Joyce and Carolee went off to rest. Rose began preparing for the night shift while Annabel straightened the room and Bethany took up her book again.

"Run really hot water in the sink and soak everything well," Rose told Annabel. "We'll let the water cool before we put our hands in, but I want to kill all the germs we can."

Bethany read aloud about the March girls' trials in *Little Women* and felt glad she could avert her eyes from the purplish, misshapen creature in front of her who no longer whooped, yet seemed no better. Shirley's breath came fast now but seemed shallow. The doctor dropped by again about nine.

"The mucous has hardened and settled lower in her lungs. She isn't contagious anymore," he told Rose, "even though her glands are still swollen and tender. Pneumonia is the prime concern, especially that fever. You had better send for your parents," he said. Rose stifled an exclamation. "Just in case," he added.

He patted Annabel's shoulder on his way out the door. "You know, sweetheart," the doctor said gravely, "when you have children, they're going to get injected so they never have to catch pertussis. And your grandchildren might get a shot to keep away mumps." He paused to consider. "Maybe when you're really old, some whippersnapper will invent an injection to fend off pneumonia."

A wave, and he was out the door, taking the quarantine sign with him. Again, Rose telephoned Evan. "I'll call your parents," he offered, "and then pick them up about ten or so. Glenn will be gone from the service station by now, and I hate to disturb Archie's parents this late. Why don't we have Glenn move home tomorrow?"

Rose agreed. "Joyce is already asleep in our bed. You might sleep in Glenn's bed tonight."

"I don't know that either of us will sleep. If we do, it will be a nap on the sofa. I'll see you soon."

Rose went back to the sickroom to gently sponge Shirley's face and hands, brush back her hair, and fetch the last of the ice. She wasn't sure Evan could get more before morning. Now and then, Shirley coughed. She slept lightly but more peacefully, and Rose realized the doctor was right. Her sister might not wake fully when their parents came.

***

Unaware of her grandparents' visit the night before, Carolee was surprised to discover her father shaving in the bathroom when she awoke to relieve Annabel and Bethany at six o'clock the next morning. Checking on her mother, she said, "I'll wake Joyce for you."

"Just a minute," Rose almost snapped, "I'm trying to understand her."

Weakly, Shirley was trying to say something and kept trying to kick off her bedding and gesturing to her legs—the shapely legs she had shown to some advantage once upon a time, even with her modest teaching wardrobe.

"You must stay covered, Shirl," Rose insisted. "You don't want to catch a chill on top of everything else."

Shirley shook her head slightly, and even that motion filled her eyes with tears. She coughed weakly.

"Your legs," Carolee guessed abruptly. "You want your legs to show?"

Minutely, Shirley nodded.

"She means *later*, Mama. Isn't that right, Aunt Shirley?"

Shirley's eyes brightened, then her lids sank in exhaustion and she slept again.

"At the visitation," Carolee whispered to her mother. Rose stared at her daughter. Her children had never seen a dying relative, let alone a viewing. But of course, Carolee read the newspaper avidly and would have seen obituaries and funeral announcements. "Her legs still look pretty," Carolee explained. "I think she wants them to show, not her swollen face."

At that, Rose looked so weary and gray that Carolee, as if she were the parent, led her mother into the bedroom to rest. Annabel went upstairs to sob into Bethany's arms.

⚷

"It was Shirley's final wish," Rose repeated to those who came to console the family and pay their respects on Sunday evening. In a petal-scented room in the mortuary, Rose's sister lay surrounded by pastel sprays of flowers, the upper body concealed by the closed section of the casket, which was topped by a spray of white roses and a hand-tinted photograph. Beyond the roses lay Shirley's lower legs, displayed resplendently in cream silk stockings. White slippers covered her feet.

Joyce had taken the bus downtown to secure the necessary items. She had also wanted to make sure she still had a job. She did. In fact, Lois seemed to like Joyce even more now that she had met Papa. Even better, she had learned that Harvey Pratt in Men's Wear hadn't bothered to chat with the girl covering for Joyce. Maybe he wasn't as fickle as everyone said. Not that Joyce felt the need to be faithful to him. She was still young and it was best to keep her options open. At the viewing, she adopted a post by the guest book so she could survey boys arriving outside and mingling inside the room. It also allowed her to avoid the casket. She couldn't believe her mother had agreed to show Shirley's legs! Joyce could count on hearing about that from the girls at church. She hoped the scandal would die down before school started.

On the other hand, she congratulated herself on how appropriate her choice of a charcoal-and-white silk dress had been for the occasion. It was too bad that Lois was the only person from work who showed up, and that she mainly spoke with Evan, after extending sympathies to Joyce and Rose. Joyce had not really expected Harvey to come, and with Shirley's legs, maybe it was just as well he hadn't. It seemed like months since she had last seen him. Her thoughts drifted to a certain apricot blouse with a lace collar that was still available on the third floor. *That would catch his eye*, she thought. She had seen a similar blouse, colored green, in last month's issue of *Ingenue* magazine. The apricot shade would suit Joyce's coloring perfectly if she could find the right lipstick to match.

She noted the local church leaders solemnly greeting her parents—the bishop, Shirley's bishop, their stake president. Even from her post by the door, she could hear enough to guess at their conversation. Aunt Shirley was at peace now, they would be saying. *We don't understand, but we accept God's will.* It reminded her of something Papa had said over dinner one night. He said the defense attorney at a trial had done "everything but stand on his head to prove his client's innocence," then changed his tune at sentencing and mentioned his client's awful childhood experiences as the reason he had been "caused to commit the crime."

After so much medical care and so much inconvenience for the family, after so many prayers and a special blessing, they now believed it had been the intended outcome all along? How did they keep a straight face?

Her thoughts were not the only ones to spiral away from the sad immediacy of the coffin to some strand of escapism. While young people ventured into the overly-perfumed room to see the once-vibrant woman who had been their teacher, Shirley's family began unconsciously to comfort, distract, reminisce, and change the subject. Beryl helped her parents settle in among some friends at the far end of the room and then moved between Rose and their brothers as if she were hosting a party. If a gap opened up between visitors, Beryl sought to close it up like she was the Boulder Dam—a massive arc of concrete holding back the water in the desert. Having done that, it even occurred to her to bring up the dam as a topic of conversation.

"I don't understand your interest," murmured Evan, "since you live in Ogden. Is it because of Floyd working for the railroad?" he asked.

"Of course," Beryl said, pausing to embrace a cluster of schoolteachers. She returned and seamlessly resumed their conversation. "I've hitched a ride in Floyd's engine several times over the last few years. It's interesting to be surrounded by lizards and sagebrush for hours and then suddenly come upon that brand new town next to the dam. Some of our friends were involved in building it."

"I heard about a scientist from the university who was down there driving a backhoe or some darn thing," Evan offered.

"Yes, it attracted a lot of people looking for work. An Ogden firm called Utah Construction was one of six companies that built the whole thing. We know a lot of people that way."

Evan clapped a hand on his son's shoulder as Glenn joined his parents at the foot of the coffin. "Is there a job available for a strapping young fellow like Glenn?" he asked. "He's nineteen now and almost twenty."

"Maybe," Beryl said. "I think the young men have moved on now, though."

"He's trying to ship me out of town," Glenn quipped, easing over to Rose's far side. He hoped to offer support without having to say much. "Sit, Mama," he whispered to his mother, but she shook her head. At least she knew he was present.

Shirley had been Glenn's first babysitter, yet even at the mortuary he tingled with inescapable flashes, not of Shirley but of his girlfriend. He couldn't stop eyeing the visitors' bodies as they soberly entered the room. It was hard to believe that people could walk around seemingly unaware of their supremely sensitive body parts! He tried to imagine that married couples might have had sex all afternoon, yet he could not detect signs of any lingering bliss beneath the mourners' sad demeanor.

He daydreamed about Margie and how delectable she

had looked and smelled that day when she squeezed into the Hudson to accompany the family to the mortuary. After the first hour, when Margie clearly had tired of being introduced to a steady stream of relatives, Evan handed Glenn the car keys and muttered, "Make it quick." Glenn had surreptitiously run her home, with only time for a kiss.

Perhaps Glenn's preoccupation with Margie was picked up somehow by the grave-faced triplets who were huddled on the loveseat. Despite the heat, they were wearing identical Christmas dresses made out of navy taffeta, with white-lace yokes. The dresses were a little short and tight under their arms. Joyce had declared their Easter dresses—made of pink, yellow, and turquoise organdies with sashes that tied in front—unsuitable for a funeral. Rose hadn't found the energy to argue.

Suddenly Bethany asked in a low voice, "What did Papa mean about mumps *falling* on boys? Where does it fall? What does it mean?"

The three of them considered this for a moment, staring at their brother as they thought, then Carolee offered an idea. "They said something about glands. It's probably not the lymph glands because everyone has those. It has to be something lower."

Silence. Then Annabel gasped and threw a hand over her mouth. "Just picture Bobby when he runs outside naked," she muttered from behind her hand.

Bethany did. It wasn't difficult because the little boy had escaped outside naked twice since the temperature had soared. "Those are *glands*?" she asked.

"The roundish part has another name—something like what octopuses have: tentacles, I think." They all broke up giggling. Across the room, their parents frowned.

Carolee smoothed her dress. "I know this much," she

82 announced softly in her most medical voice, "those *glands* on boys must have something to do with making babies. *That's* why Glenn can't catch the mumps. I bet you each a Tootsie Pop."

"How are we going to find out to collect?" Annabel asked scornfully. "I think we should just assume all that extra stuff boys have has some purpose."

"Like easy peeing during a hike," Bethany suggested. With hands clasped over their giggles, they had to seek refuge in the hall. There they located a drinking fountain and took long, calming turns. In the drinking fountain's gurgle, Bethany thought she could hear the sound of boys peeing. She thought she could hear Aunt Shirley laughing too.

seven

Though they all mourned Shirley's passing, her illnesses had been so exhausting that now the sense of relief seemed to lighten their moods. The sickroom became the dining room again, where the triplets wanted to keep the rug rolled up so they could practice their tap dance for the ward talent show in August. Their shuffles and kicks alternated with Joyce's rehearsal of a Gershwin medley, and the house became noisy again. Only Rose remained quiet.

The Fourth of July observance was lost to the funeral, so Evan figured Covered Wagon Days would be an easy compensation for the children. It was officially the twenty-fourth of July, but since it fell on a Sunday this year, the arrival of the Mormon pioneers would be celebrated on Monday the twenty-fifth. Evan arranged to go to the station late so the family could stroll through the park in the morning, see the conclusion of the parade, and have a picnic.

He suggested a family outing before then, but Rose insisted that she was not up to it. Every evening it seemed Evan found her shifting through lengths of fabric or her basket of trim but not really focusing on any project. Well, he could at least get her a little time to herself, he decided. He asked for a day off work and purchased eight tickets for the train to Saltair. He watched the glee in his children's eyes as he handed the tickets around at dinner, even awarding Glenn and Joyce two tickets each.

"I thought you each might want to ask a friend," he explained, watching their faces brighten.

"Why can't we ask friends?" Annabel complained.

"Six ten-year-olds?" Joyce began scornfully, but stopped when her father shook his head. The question was moot and everyone knew it.

"May we go swimming?" Carolee requested.

"You can get wet," Evan said, "but you can't swim because it's too salty. If you splash, you get salt in your eyes. You can float, though. I'll rent suits for you and you can change as soon as you get out. We don't need any more illness in this house."

Joyce shuddered at the thought of wearing a bathing suit that someone else had worn recently. "No thanks, I'll take my own along," she said. Actually, she remembered, she had seen a stunning navy maillot just yesterday.

"Fine, just bring something to carry it around in wet," Evan said, unaware of how much experience his eldest daughter had in transporting extra clothing.

"Can we ride on the giant racer? And the big ferris wheel?" Bethany coaxed.

"We'll do all we can do until it gets too hot," Evan promised. "Everyone plan to wear a hat, and Glenn will find the canteens. Let's catch an early train, right after you girls finish in the garden, so we won't have to contend with the evening crowd. You kids can have your fun now, and later this summer your mother and I will go back to Saltair to dance." He glanced at his wife. "They still have the best big band in the state."

Rose rewarded him with a smile. Before the triplets were born, they had often gone dancing at Saltair.

"I think I'll invite Peggy," Joyce said. "We can steal Margie away from Glenn and have some fun."

"Fat chance," Glenn muttered.

When the day came, they chose to sit in the open railway cars on the ride due west, Annabel beside Evan, Carolee and Bethany in the facing seats. Ahead of them, the teenaged girls chatted animatedly while Evan tried not to notice that Glenn and Margie couldn't seem to keep their hands off each other, even in public. He reminded himself to continue to restrict Glenn's access to the family car and to make sure his son registered for classes in auto mechanics in the fall. Clearly, Glenn was determined to grow up fast.

Margie seemed just short of being flirtatious with Evan as she tried to win his approval. He had to admit that she was charming, but the poor child had never really known a father and likely didn't know how to behave around an older man. *Is that what I am now, an older man?* he thought. *I'm over forty. I was barely legal when Glenn was born.* He stared at the landscape creeping past and sighed. Life seemed to go by a lot quicker these days.

There was not much to see as they clattered past miles of sage and salt. He told the girls that Black Rock, which they would see jutting out of the lake near the resort, had attracted Brigham Young and his pioneers. "When they celebrated one year in the valley, they took their families out there in a wagon train—a kind of parade. Well, that would be a pretty long parade, I guess. They liked to picnic and float in the Great Salt Lake, just like we're going to do. They even slept on the beach.

By the tenth year, though, they figured out it was better to celebrate a summer holiday up in the canyon."

"You're making this up," Carolee accused.

"Cross my heart, kiddo. Your mother's family camped out with them. Once the railroad was built in 1869, even rich people from the east came here, all dressed up in fancy suits and bustles. The train reached Salt Lake in 1870 and made it to the resort in the 1890s. One of the country's presidents visited Saltair, but I forget which one. There were a couple of steamships on the lake that sailed around Antelope Island to give tourists a show."

"Did they ride the giant racer?" Bethany asked.

"Not back then, but that roller coaster is so rickety, you could believe it was that old."

Evan soon ran out of history and had to involve the triplets in spotting jackrabbits—or anything that moved in the distance—out the window. They spied a hawk swooping down to seize a rattlesnake less than fifty yards from the tracks, which made the girls squeal. Soon everyone in the car was straining to look. The older girls joined in the gasps as the snake twisted and fought in the hawk's talons; but the raptor swooped, climbed, and vanished into the clouds. Finally the Moorish outline of the Saltair pavilion appeared, and the restless waves glittered with sun and salt. The triplets bounced as if they were doing jumping jacks until the train pulled into the station.

After arranging a meeting place to catch the five o'clock train home, Evan turned the teenagers loose, their hands full of tickets, and took the younger girls for an hour in the brine. Afterward they had hot dogs and root beer for lunch. Once the girls deemed which rides were adventurous enough to deserve their tickets, they settled on a fair system of rotating who sat by a sister on each ride and who got the coveted seat by their father. The giant racer proved to be their favorite. Riding it again and again, they all went hoarse from screaming. Evan felt his bones ache from the girls hanging onto him.

"Hey, I've had more strain on my arm today than when I took a bullet," he teased them.

They straggled back to the train station to see Margie show off a giant teddy bear Glenn had won for her in the shooting gallery. On the train Margie still held the bear proudly in her lap, while Joyce and Peggy chatted about clothes and the triplets extended their new shiny pinwheels out the windows to catch the breeze.

"Taste your skin," Carolee said to her sisters, touching her tongue to her shoulder. "We're like pretzels coated with salt."

If they had not nodded off, Evan later told Rose, the triplets would have disgusted all the passengers by licking their own skin all the way back to the city.

As his younger daughters napped, Evan mused about the strange disappearance of Pearlann Jones. Her parents had called again. The wedding invitations she'd handed out at church nagged him. Ward members had been quietly told that the wedding was a fantasy. Pearlann suffered some kind of brain damage at birth and had the body of a woman and the mental age of someone younger than the triplets. What bothered Evan most was that she'd disappeared on the day she thought she was going to be married. What were the odds of that?

They had interviewed the pretend groom, Ronald Johnston, more than once. His mental abilities were almost as impaired as Pearlann's were. His parents confirmed that he had eaten dinner and had gone to bed as usual that day. Evan wondered if Pearlann's fantasy had taken her aboard a Greyhound bus. Maybe she had ended up in Pocatello or Redding and was too confused to contact her parents, let alone make her way home.

Drowsily he gazed at his daughters curled opposite him as if they were infants again. He could feel the sweat from Bethany's forehead soak through his slacks. Margie's head had found Glenn's shoulder. Joyce and Peggy still talked softly. Rearing a family wasn't easy during bad economic times. Having triplets posed additional challenges, he mused, even though he still considered himself to be a lucky son-of-a-gun.

When he returned to work the next day, he was back on the Frankie Stuart case while one of the detectives took vacation. The case had cooled since the initial heat when the boy's description first hit the radio and newspapers. Recently, Frankie's mother had told a reporter her son might have accompanied an aunt on a trip through the Northwest. Astounded by this casual speculation, the detectives shook their heads in wariness about whether the boy had even been abducted. Maybe Mrs. Stuart had just lost track of him, either by accident or design.

Perry Beale, the other detective on the case, filled Evan in on the latest developments. "Traveling Aunt Jewel is back in Salt Lake, and I think she's as balmy as Frankie's mother."

"No sign of Frankie?" Evan asked.

"Not a whiff. The woman says she would never take Frankie that far. She says he's too much of a handful. Anyway, she didn't even know the boy was missing."

Evan frowned. "So this little kid is seen at Liberty Park by the elephant trainer and maybe by the guy who runs the merry-go-round, and all the while his mother thinks he's taking a nap or maybe traveling two or three states away with his aunt?"

"Yeah, well, it doesn't help that his mother is two-thirds through a bottle of cheap gin by noon." Beale raked his hand through his dark crew cut. "Is this how people take care of their kids these days?"

"It makes you wonder. I see children running down the sidewalk or playing in the park without any adult in sight, and I can't help think how easy it would be for someone to grab them. Do we have any reasonably good suspects?"

"I'm coming back to the elephant guy, if you want to know," Detective Beale said. "What's his name, Stucki?"

"Stuka. Hugo. Thing is, there are people around that elephant enclosure all day. He doesn't have the means or opportunity, and I don't know about motive. My triplets know him, and he's never pulled anything funny. I questioned them a few weeks ago."

"Maybe he fed Frankie to the elephant. The high cost of feed would be his motive."

"Right," Evan said dryly. "Maybe Princess Alice confused him for a peanut. What about the deadbeat father? He doesn't seem to have an alibi, does he?"

"Naw, but that's almost too easy. The guy says he was help-ing a friend move to Moab, and the sheriff out there couldn't find any proof one way or the other." Beale picked up his sport coat. "So, where do you want to start?"

"With the mom. It's only ten o'clock, so maybe she's still sober." Evan strapped on his holster. "Any reason to update the press?"

"Why? Let's face it, the kid's gone. We've got zero. Nobody's going to spot him now. This one will probably be solved by deer hunters."

Evan flinched as put on his coat. He hated to think of a kid crumpled up in the underbrush in one of the canyons. By autumn, they would find bones, mostly.

Rose let the triplets help sort through her latest collection of trimmings while Joyce picked through lengths of fabric and settled on a stretch of black jersey. "I'd really like this for a tunic," Joyce said. "There isn't enough for a dress."

"It's too old for you," Rose responded. "I don't like seeing young girls dressed in black. What about a straight skirt with kick pleats?"

"That might work." Joyce stood in her parents' bedroom and draped the fabric around her. "We already have a pattern for that."

"Thank goodness for a friend like Doris," Rose said. "I hardly get around to the sales anymore and she's so good at picking out ends of bolts for us. It seems like cute trimming is so pricey anymore!"

"Why shop if you have a friend in a fabric store?" Joyce said, suddenly wondering why she had never made it to the Fabric Department of the ZCMI store.

"Mama, we have to buy tap shoes before the talent show," Annabel put in as she considered a strip of daisy cut-outs. "That's less than a month from now."

"Not a chance," Rose said. "They're too expensive, and you'd outgrow them in a jiffy."

"But no one will hear us tapping!" Still seated, she demonstrated in her sandals. "We might as well dance barefoot and break our toes. That could cost *more* than tap shoes."

"We'll put taps on your new Easter shoes," Rose countered.

"Your toes are already pushing toward the ends of your old ones, and you need new ones before school, so that way we'll kill two birds with one stone."

"You're not planning on doing the 'I Get a Kick Out of You' routine again, are you?" Joyce asked archly. "You've just about worn out that cute little threesome bit."

They shrugged off her comment and rewarded her with an impromptu performance, high-kicking in turn, and narrowly missing one another.

"We aren't doing that one," Bethany said, panting slightly, "but how would you know? You're never here to play the piano for us."

Joyce rolled her eyes. "I thought Margie was. She's here all the time when I'm at work. I suppose she's too busy with our big brother."

"Margie doesn't play piano," Annabel said, "but she's seen our routine. It's something new, unless you've seen the Broadway show. Our dance teacher learned it from a friend who dances at the University of Utah."

"Which show?" Rose asked.

"It's from *Porgy and Bess*," Carolee offered. "In September our class will see the entire play at Kingsbury Hall. I bet Lorraine's friend will perform in it."

"Joyce, why don't you sew our costumes?" Bethany suggested excitedly. "We're doing 'I Got Plenty o' Nuttin'.' You could make us hobo costumes."

"I don't have time," their sister said, folding the jersey and setting it aside. "I need every spare minute to practice Gershwin."

"I like the hobo idea," their mother chimed in. "I have enough material from your sundresses to make pouches you could hang on sticks."

"Our sundresses are new," Carolee said. "That won't look right for hobos."

"It's all right. We'll baste on a patch or two. You can't look *too* ragged or your new Easter shoes will look out of place."

Annabel sighed. "I'd like real tap shoes some day," she said. "When I'm rich, I'm going to buy three pair: one white, one black, and one red."

"I'm going to practice the piano right now while I'm thinking about it," Joyce announced. "You can practice when I'm finished."

"Let's see if we have enough of that paper-doll fabric for pouches," Rose suggested.

Carolee went to check the scrap drawer in the linen closet while her two sisters took a turn sorting the new fabric for school clothes. Rose wondered if a bolt of navy corduroy might make three skirts, while the girls set about finding complementary blouse material.

Evan was pleased to find Rose engaged with sewing that evening after his daughters had wandered off. He wasn't in the mood for cheerful banter with children. He sat down and devoured a plate of cold cuts. Rose noticed her husband's brooding disposition. She turned her chair away from the sewing machine for a moment so she could face him and asked, "What is it, Evan? Why don't you tell me while I stuff these hobo pouches."

"You're making pouches for hobos?"

"For your daughters, actually. It's for their talent show. I also have a skirt for Carolee that I need to pin."

Carolee heard her name as she left the bathroom, so she tiptoed through the kitchen to listen at the dining room door.

"We don't have any leads," her father was saying, "but the Frankie Stuart case is as hinky as all get out."

"I thought he was traveling with a relative."

"The relative is back and there's no joy there. The thing is, if a kid that small wanders off, anyone could stick him into the back seat of a car and be in another state before anyone knew he was gone."

"What do you think happened?"

"I don't know. That's the trouble. It would make sense if we found a bad guy who knew the boy, but absent that, I think I'm liking the estranged husband for this one."

Rose gasped so sharply that Carolee jumped. As her father's voice dropped, Carolee edged a few inches closer. "It's easy for someone to kill a child without meaning to," he explained. "Say the little guy wouldn't stop whining and the father over-reacted."

Rose shuddered. "That reminds me of a strange dream I had last night. Someone opened a big drawer to show me some babies all dressed up and tucked away in the bureau."

"Like in a morgue?"

"Not exactly. They were sleeping. It's still odd to put them in a drawer."

Carolee didn't need to hear any more before scooting through the kitchen and upstairs. "I know what happened to Frankie Stuart," she said.

"How can you know that," said Bethany.

"I heard Papa say his strange father killed him."

"His father?"

"His *strange* father. Maybe by accident."

"Don't say that," Annabel cringed.

Carolee's eyes sparkled. "I have a hunch he's buried him in their vegetable garden." She paused and added, "Do you think they have a vegetable garden?"

"Everyone does," Bethany sighed.

"Tonight," Carolee whispered, "let's sneak over and dig him up."

"Ick," said Annabel. "That would make me throw up. He'd be all chopped up like the meat we had in the salad for dinner."

"Frankie bits!" Carolee squealed and then teamed with Bethany to tickle Annabel.

Downstairs the telephone rang. Grabbing the receiver, Evan spoke briefly and then hung up. "I have to go back to work."

"What—now? Tonight?"

"I'm afraid so." He added grimly, "I guess it's just as well I postponed our vacation. By the way, my theory on Frankie was wrong."

"What happened, Evan?"

"Another child from the same neighborhood is missing. Her name is Mary Agnes Malone."

Earlier that evening, Sol and Mary Agnes were engaging in a third game of checkers. "How about a root beer float?" Sol had asked, jumping three of her pieces at once.

"Cheater! Okay, I love root beer floats. But you still cheat!" She fingered the fringe on the Peter Pan outfit she was wearing, where it ruffled above her knee. "Are you giving this costume to me? It fits perfectly."

"No, my mother bought that for me when I was young. I thought you might like to try it on."

"Crown me, finally. Were you Peter Pan on Halloween?"

"You bet. A couple of years in a row. My mother used to say I could be her little boy forever." He jumped two more black checkers, then got to his feet.

"No fair! I better go home. I bet my mother is calling me."

"Have a root beer float first. I'll fix it while you take off the Peter Pan outfit. I don't want you to spill ice cream on it."

"Okay, but I'm not supposed to cross Seventh East after dark."

From the kitchen Sol heard Mary Agnes using the bathroom. Good, he thought. By the time she drank the last of her root beer, she was going to feel sleepy. He lifted the telephone off the hook and made sure she could hear him replace it.

"Here you go," he said, setting down the glass with a flourish. "Guess what? Your mother says you can spend the night."

"Did not!"

"Sure she did. I called while you were in the bathroom. Enjoy your root beer float and then I'll show you a secret I have in my storage space. See that little trap door?" He lowered his voice and stared into her eyes. "No one on earth knows what's up there."

Mary Agnes pretended to consider. "A big secret or a little secret?" she asked.

About sunrise, Evan drove home for a shower and couple hours of sleep, but decided to take a detour when he saw Hugo Stuka entering the park from Seventh East. He parked by the main gate. He could feel fatigue in his hips and knees from not having slept as he walked to the barn. It wasn't as easy to pull off all-nighters as it had once been.

"Don't come in here," Stuka called over the elephant's rumbles as Evan's shadow fell across the doorway. "I'll be out directly."

Waiting, Evan drew a fist over his sandpapery eyelids. His brain replayed the facts like a scratched recording. Two children missing from adjoining neighborhoods. A four-year-old boy and then a girl twice that age. It didn't make sense. They didn't look alike, they were different ages and genders. Would the same person abduct both or were they looking for two offenders?

Emerging into the early sunlight, Stuka carefully studied the flyer Evan handed him. "Another child? That's horrible! I think I've seen this girl around. Is she real skinny?"

"She is. Her mother said the photograph is a couple years old. When did you last see her?"

Stuka looked again. "Is this the girl I'm thinking of? If so, she's not always, how should I say, very clean. She's uncombed, maybe."

"Mary Agnes is the same year in school as my girls. I think you know my triplets."

"Yes, but your girls look cared for, even if they've skinned a knee playing. This one—Mary Agnes, did you say?—not so much. Kind of grimy, like she doesn't bathe very often."

Evan thought for a minute. "Do you know my girls' names?"

"I know Bethany, who comes most often. And isn't one of them called Annabel? I remember because my wife's name is Anna." A pause. "Your other girl, who looks like Annabel," he said while gesturing to indicate braids, "I don't recall her name."

"Do you know the name of the little boy who has gone missing? He's the one we asked you about."

"Yes, that boy I thought was a girl. I didn't know his name, but you or your partner said it yesterday. Frankie, is that right?"

A switch flipped in Evan's brain. *Of course: a little boy who looks like a girl. I ought to mention it to Beale. Maybe we're tracking a typical pedophile, after all. Maybe the cuss just isn't too particular about age.*

"Mr. Stuka, did you ever see Frankie and Mary Agnes

together, holding hands or sharing peanuts for the elephant—
anything like that?"

"No, this girl, if she's the one I'm thinking of, is never with
anyone. She hangs around the edges, you know?"

"When did you last see her?"

Another pause. "So many children come to see the elephant," Stuka apologized. "One day, another day, the next—"
He shrugged. From inside the barn, the elephant bellowed.

Evan thanked him and again left his card. "If you think of
anything, please call."

"I will. And I'll ask Princess Alice. You know, she likes the
children. Sometimes elephants are smarter than people."

Evan couldn't help but wonder how the elephant might
communicate anything to her handler. *I'd hate to see her on the
witness stand!* He was getting punchy. Starting the car, he realized he would consider almost anyone as a suspect by now.

As he rounded the perimeter near Ninth South to head
home, sun flashed from under the leaves and he nearly crowded
a girl on horseback off the road. The horse shied to the right.
Evan moved to the left and pulled over. He got out to find the
girl soothing her horse.

"Sorry," he said, hurrying through the dust. "Are you all
right? I didn't mean to come up on you like that."

"I'm fine," she said swinging out of the saddle. "I'm not
used to traffic so early. We were probably out in the middle of
the road."

"Are you here often?"

Nora Taylor explained about exercising horses. No, she didn't
recognize the missing girl from the grainy photograph, she said.

"She lives right over on Thirteenth South. Do you ever ride
down that way?"

"Yes, that's my route, both to and from the stable, but I hardly ever see children. I'm here when the sun is coming up and try to get the horses back before it gets hot. I guess it's too early."

"Do you see anyone hanging around in the park or near it?"

"Only the people who work in the zoo—and my brother who teaches tennis. I see folks watering their lawns or gardening sometimes when I'm on my way back."

"Maybe you could keep my card and call if you see Mary Agnes or notice anything out of the ordinary. Anything at all."

"I'll do that. I hope you find her."

As he pulled away, Evan watched the girl—Nora, she said her name was—in his rear-view mirror. She seemed to be a bright kid and an excellent rider. Maybe she would remember something. He ran a hand over his stubbly jaw and thought that a couple hours of sleep would do, then a quick clean-up before going back to the station.

As he waited to turn onto Thirteenth South, he noticed a girl in a wheelchair across the street and remembered he had seen her seated beneath the willow tree before. She must spend considerable time watching the street, he thought. The missing children had both tended to wander, so maybe she had seen them. When he drove across Thirteenth and pulled into the driveway, a woman immediately came out of the house as if she had been watching. She introduced herself as Amelia Schatz and took him across the lawn to meet Lara.

He showed them his flyer. Lara made an upward movement with her hand, palm showing.

"That means yes," Miss Schatz said, sounding surprised. "I don't recognize the girl, but a bunch of children live around here."

Lara was sketching rapidly with her left hand, her right hand weighting the sketch pad.

"You draw well," Evan said.

"She's always had a talent." Amelia explained about Lara's immigration and her nerve disease.

Lara looked up, and Evan took the sketch pad. A rumpled girl appeared to be playing hopscotch.

"You've seen her out playing?" Yes.

"Where was her hopscotch? In the park?" No.

"On the sidewalk?" Another yes.

Evan gazed the length of the block at unremarkable bungalows and cottages. "Was the hopscotch by a particular house?"

Lara shrugged slightly.

"Did you see her get into a car or see anyone force her to come with them?" Negative.

Evan glanced at his watch, thanked them, and appropriated the sketch. The captain had called a meeting, presumably to tell them why two missing children was worse than one and that it was a pattern, likely indicating someone from the state, not a drifter just passing through.

Evan rehearsed in his mind how he would add that because the children were picked up from roughly the same neighborhood, the perpetrator must live there too. And something else. Both of the children seemed to have been neglected by their parents. Maybe the case didn't have anything to do with Liberty Park. He would tell the uniformed officers about the handicapped girl, Lara, who sat and watched everything from her spot under a willow tree.

Two things haunted Evan. First of all, the children had been taken at around six weeks apart. That meant that before summer's end, it was likely another child would disappear.

100   Second, he didn't buy the drifter theory any longer. He felt
almost certain they were hunting a predator who lived somewhere nearby.

eight

Margie barely made it back into bed before her mother started screaming at her. She practically sat down on top of Margie, who had turned her face into her pillow. "You might as well tell me!" Darlene yelled. "You're late, aren't you! And you're sicker than a cat with a fur ball."

Margie gagged at the image and turned her face up a bit for air. "Go to work."

"It's Sunday. I'd be sleeping in except for hearing someone retching in the bathroom."

"I'm going back to sleep. Leave me alone," Margie pleaded.

But Darlene wouldn't quit. "What do you care if it's Sunday? You don't have a job anyway! Listen here, no more freeloading, sister. If you're knocked up, do you think those prim so-and-sos at the high school are going to let you back in?"

"I'm not pregnant."

"Yes you are. And don't think you're moving that boy Glenn *or his kid* in here with me!"

Margie squeezed her eyes tightly, but the room had begun to rotate. She clenched the sheet for balance and drew up her knees, hoping she wouldn't vomit again.

"I have to pay rent here, you know. You didn't bother to even get a summer job. There's no room here for a boyfriend."

Margie decided not to comment. Darlene feared little, but she did care what the neighbors thought of her allowing Creep to spend so much time at the house and never let him stay the night.

"Why don't you just admit you're knocked up?"

"You are *so* crude! I have a touch of the flu, is all. Maybe I'm coming down with polio, so leave me alone and let me sleep it off."

"You won't sleep *this off*, missy, and your boyfriend isn't going to sleep it off either. You need to tell him the facts of life or I'll call his parents. In fact, I'm calling right now." A pause. "What's Glenn's last name?"

"I won't tell you! Just leave me alone. I'll see him later. Right now, his whole family is at church anyway."

Darlene snorted as she stormed from the room. Margie buried her face in her pillow again. She couldn't be pregnant, she told herself. Even if she were, pregnancy couldn't possibly feel this awful. Her breasts felt swollen and sore, as if her period would start any minute. She had never been so exhausted in her entire life.

I probably do have polio. Please, God, don't let me get paralyzed. Don't let my legs shrink to just bones.

If she was coming down with polio, she hoped she would die fast—or be a miracle girl, maybe get her picture in the newspapers. *That would show Darlene!*

Besides, she and Glenn had only done it a few times, and every single time they had, she had cleaned herself up. How often had she heard that girls got caught because they didn't take care of themselves? She *couldn't* be pregnant. She rolled against the wall. "I'm not pregnant," she whispered. Within minutes, she fell into a slumber that felt as vast and cloudy as the current summer sky.

The following day Margie's worries continued to trouble her, as if she had just spent an evening in a nest of red ants that were stinging her brain. She haltingly confided in Helen, who quickly told Irene. Bound by a prism of emotion, the three friends waited.

⚷

While Mary Agnes enjoyed her crunchy sardine sandwich (it was crunchier due to the pulverized pills hiding within the fish), Sol gave Frankie an old shirt and shorts from storage and then hunted out a baseball cap to cover the boy's fair curls. He ran a tepid bath for the boy and added dish soap for bubbles. Bathtubs proved useful in so many ways.

"Let's play a game," Sol suggested, soaping away the hardened grime on the boy's scalp and cheerfully moving on. "Look what a dirty birdie Frankie is today."

"Ouch! Stop washing me. Stop, I said!"

"I'm a wizard, and I'm washing a-way Fran—kie! No more Frankie. B-z-z-l-l-t! All gone."

Frankie felt for his wet locks, checked between his thighs, then patted his feet. He looked relieved. "No washing away!"

"I'm a wizard! I'm turn-ing dirty Fran-kie in-to a clean boy named Fred-dy."

"No Freddy!"

"Be-cause *Fred-dy* gets to go to Li-ber-ty Park!"

The boy's eyes brightened. Silence. The last time he went outside, they merely played catch in the narrow backyard.

"If dirty Frankie comes back, he has to take a nap. But Freddy gets to go to the park!"

"I can play Freddy. You can be Wizard."

"Good for you, Freddy. Now stand up and let me take a good look at you."

Sol also took a peek into the kitchen, expecting protest from another quarter. Mary Agnes was still chewing, but by now she was supporting her head with one hand. "Mary Agnes!" he called. She looked up through leaden eyelids. "Finish that bite and then go curl up on my bed where it's cool. Hurry, you lucky girl." He didn't especially want to carry her.

He turned his attention back to drying and dressing the boy. This was the first time he had let them both come downstairs, and perhaps it would be the last. He didn't like to take chances. In fact, Mary Agnes smarted off so freely that he might soon send her on a long bus ride to the end of the line—with a crunchy sardine sandwich. A last-run-of-the-day bus ride as far as he could send her. The trouble was, she knew his name and where he lived. He wondered if any buses ran up the canyons. For now, back to the business at hand.

"Freddy, I'm going to let you borrow my baseball cap. You don't want to sunburn your nose."

"No baseball cap."

"Oh dear. I think that's the bad dirty Frankie coming back. Do you want to ride the carousel or not?"

"Do!"

"Then hold still and let me wipe your nose. See, the keen thing about this hat is that your hair won't get so messy. Isn't that peachy keen?"

"Peachy, not keen."

Sol chuckled. "Okay, the park is a big place, so we have to

practice. Pretend you get lost and I find you. I say, 'What's your name, little boy?'"

"Peachy."

"Oh dear. I guess Freddy doesn't want to ride the carousel."

"Do!"

"We can't if you're not going to behave. Let's try it again. 'Hello, little boy. What's your name?'"

"Freddy."

"Say *Freddy Niessen*. What's your name? Freddy what?"

"Freddy Niessen."

"Good boy! And who am I?"

"Wizard."

"How about 'Uncle Sol?' Maybe we can even ride the ferris wheel. Would you like that, Freddy?" He checked the high latch on the back door.

"No!"

Sol led the boy out the front door, tightly gripping his hand, locking the door behind them. "You really don't like the ferris wheel? That big circle that goes around and around like this?"

"No, too scary!"

"Okay, we don't have to ride the ferris wheel. Maybe we can go to the playground if you are a very good boy."

Once in the park, Sol took the youngster by the shoulders and turned him around. "Let's play getting lost again, Freddy. Where do you live, little boy?"

"That way." He pointed across Thirteenth South.

"Wonderful, Freddy."

"Who brought you to the park today?"

"Sol-face."

"Uncle Sol. Say it: Uncle Sol."

The boy complied, then they walked in silence, Sol holding

the boy's hand. "I think there's an airplane ride over by the carousel. Do you want to ride on the planes? They're not scary."

"The zoo!" He tugged at Sol's hand, pointing at the admission gate. "I want to go to the zoo."

"We can do that if you hold my hand all the time. Are you going to hold my hand, Freddy? Okay."

Sol paid admission and they began walking by the exhibits. In a few minutes, the crush of visitors began to make Sol uneasy. He came here often but not with this particular child, so he wondered if someone might notice him. He saw a flyer with Mary Agnes's face on it and almost panicked. Surely a flyer for Frankie hung around the next corner. He was glad he had thought of the hat.

"This is too far to walk, Freddy. I'm getting tired, and you have short little legs. Let's see one more animal and then we'll go find the carousel. Which animal do you want to see the most?"

"The elephant."

"Figures," Sol muttered. The elephant exhibit was around the curve. It likely drew the most visitors. Basically, the two of them were going to tread the entire zoo and everyone would see them. He peered between shoulders ahead, peering a ways down the path.

"How about an ostrich, Freddy? Let's go see the ostrich instead, and then we'll find some popcorn."

"No!" Suddenly the boy threw himself into the dust. "I want my mommy," he bawled. "Mom-my!"

Sol set him on his feet. "Frankie, stop," he whispered, bending to brush him off. "Stop right now!" The boy kicked him in the shin. Sol raised his hand to whack him, then remembered where he was. "You deserve a good smack," he muttered. Frankie wailed louder. Sol worried that someone might remember seeing this. Sure as anything, some bossy, do-good type might even try to intervene.

"Mommy doesn't want you to cry, Freddy," he said, trying to sound reasonable. "Do you think Mommy would want you to cry when you are so lucky to get to go to the zoo?" He pulled out his handkerchief and reluctantly began blotting salt water and mucous. "Listen, Freddy, let's go see the elephant, okay?"

The boy shrugged and scuffed his shoe, sensing the power he had when there were people around. He refused to take Sol's hand and looked as if he might take off running.

Enough of this! Let him run! Who cares?

Then the image of a small hand pointing across Thirteenth South came to mind—a small hand pointing at Sol's own house.

"Hey, do you want to ride on my shoulders, Freddy-boy? I bet that would make you as tall as the elephant." Quickly, he lifted the boy onto his shoulders and clutched him firmly. "Okay, Freddy. Do you want to see the elephant? Or ride the carousel? Or go back and take a nap?"

"Elephant first."

"Okay, don't wiggle and fall on your head."

Sol took a long breath and started walking. The kid was heavy. Across the way a young girl whined and tried to run away. He felt better. Why should anyone remember a particular little boy among all the other misbehaving brats?

Children! he thought. *How did anybody tolerate them?* Well, there was always that last bus at sunset. There would be just the two of them, Sol and little Freddy. After Freddy konked out on the back seat, Uncle Sol would vanish through the back door and that would be that. He hadn't really decided yet if that was the way it would play out.

Evan met briefly with Detective Beale after their frustrated captain strode away and the uniformed officers left for their assignments. "Still not much to go on," Beale said. "No real suspects bothering kids, no mode of transportation, no vehicle idling around playgrounds, no bodies turning up."

"Nothing tangible," Evan agreed.

"Who needs *tangible*, Flynn? Let's consult a clairvoyant or search for a trail of dropped crumbs," he said, cracking up.

Annoyed, Evan clapped his colleague on the shoulder rather vigorously. "We have a pattern, though, a sketch of the next crime: two waifs, same neighborhood, one abductor. Maybe the lack of evidence for a vehicle means there wasn't one. Maybe no bodies means the kids are still alive. Maybe the lack of suspects means it's someone who blends in and lives near the park."

"Yeah, and maybe someone does an organ recital because they can't afford a piano. Wanna grab a hamburger in Sugar House?"

"Sure, but let's drive separately. Afterward I want to check back with the girl in the wheelchair. No sense holding you up."

"Nope, she's all yours."

Evan suspected that Lara would feel freer if Beale weren't present. After lunch, he revved his engine impatiently at a red light. It was a juvenile impulse, he knew, and he didn't even have his kids in the car to appreciate it. *Okay, so I haven't quite grown up*, he said to himself. If he caught Glenn doing that, he would be furious with him.

Of course, it was Beale he was feeling impatient with, not the woman in the car ahead of him. Why couldn't Beale appreciate the value of the testimony they might elicit from the handicapped girl, Lara. If they asked her the right question, she might provide a clue as to what had happened. And reading the intangibles was what detective work was all about, wasn't it? As far as Evan believed, you pressed a question and then watched for a shift in the suspect's stance, a bouncing knee, a faraway glance, or you read the meaning of his determined stare straight into your eyes. You gave your suspect a way to save face by confessing.

Welcomed by Amelia into a dim dining room, Evan took a seat but declined coffee while the women finished lunch. Lara's sketch pad lay at his end of the table. "May I?" Evan asked.

The open page showed the beginnings of a park scene. Glancing out the window, he noted that the trees he could see were the same ones depicted in the scene. In the sketch, two figures walked away from the artist: a boy in a floppy cap and a young adult bending toward the child as if conversing while holding his hand.

"Lara was working on that when I told her it was time for lunch."

Evan smiled. "Anything unusual about these two?" No, she gestured. "Was the child crying or struggling—anything like that?"

The girl repeated the gesture and shrugged slightly. Evan turned the page and then kept turning.

Somehow he felt displaced while he gazed at her sketches of a place that was rife with high barbed-wire fences and snarling dogs. On one page, well-appointed families awaited a train, but their faces were desperate with misery. Their hands clutched carpetbags or held onto an elderly relative's arm or a child's shoulder. He thought it was odd that the soldiers were directing the people toward boxcars rather than to the passenger trains Europe was so famous for.

Evan cast Lara an inquiring look. "Is this something you read about or is it make-believe?"

"In Germany," Amelia said tightly, "my nephew works in a police office run by Herr Himmler, that little man with the spectacles. You see him standing near Adolf Hitler in the newsreels."

Evan nodded. "Why a freight train?"

"Himmler's job is to export unwanted people."

Lara seems awfully young for world politics, Evan thought. He turned another page. Here was a scene set in a leafy, wooded area. A group of people was getting off a bus, accompanied by nurses. Some of the women in uniforms and hats pushed patients' wheelchairs, yet the people they were herding were not military casualties or even refugees. He looked closely and saw that one or two of the figures seemed to be physically deformed but that most of them had the round face and drooly grin of mongoloids. In the foreground a young girl clutched a sweater around herself, her face distracted by some inward fright. In the lower right corner, a man in a white coat motioned the group toward what looked like the porch of a mansion. Perhaps it was a place that had been requisitioned as a hospital.

Evan looked questioningly at Lara, who reached for the pad.

"My nephew writes of this," Amelia offered. "Himmler's men are gathering up the infirm and having them brought to processing centers."

Lara was writing on the reverse side of that page. She pushed it toward him. "I was in that line," she had jotted. "My brother writes that I am lucky."

Evan sighed and closed the sketch pad. "Yes, I think you're lucky to be out of there. Maybe, though, the doctors are helping those people by bringing them to the right place for special treatment." His mind searched for the kind of treatment that might aid the elderly, the retarded, the insane, and sharp-minded patients like Lara. He found none.

It didn't matter, for at the moment both women stared at him, frozen by the impact of his words. "I'm sorry, did I say something wrong?"

"Gunther writes that *special treatment* is what they call the camps in Eastern Europe where they're sending the Jews," Amelia said.

Evan didn't know what to say. Clearly, these women were concerned about madness in Europe, not the two children who had gone missing from their neighborhood.

Feeling chilled, he thanked them for their time and beat a hasty retreat. He relished the exuberant heat that enveloped him on the porch and smiled at the sound of animal snorts and bleats that wafted that way from the zoo. As hopeless as the Depression was, he couldn't imagine categorizing, selecting, and shipping hordes of people off by bus or freight train to some distant location.

A quick scan around him revealed no young men or little boys, no children at all, in fact. He glanced at his watch. *It must be nap time for the little ones.*

By Saturday, Margie was checking her underpants at least hourly for blood. This must be what her English teacher called *irony.* How often had she vainly hoped her period would *not* start? She would like to trade those anxious hours when she had something important to do for the current results, when her body seemed to be signaling that everything was normal when it wasn't. Now the onset of a period would indicate nor-malcy and would change everything, change the rest of her life.

That evening when Glenn took her to a movie downtown, she could barely meet his eyes. She felt herself blush, as she imagined their private acts must have been spotlighted for everyone in the theater to know. They were probably picturing her with her legs wide, she thought, and him with his—oh, she couldn't bear it! Her sore breasts tingled as she stumbled down the dark aisle to the restroom. She glanced down and noticed a grease spot on the bodice of her blue dress. That hadn't shown up when she had pressed the dress! Now she felt even more conspicuous, branded.

Please God, please. You know everything. You must know how it feels to be seventeen and so scared.

In the bathroom she waited for an empty stall. With shaking hands, she pulled away her clothes and found nothing again. She needed the restroom anyway. She seemed to have peed ten gallons today.

In the theater it was dark, but she had counted the rows back to their seats. Glenn was laughing at the screen. He reached up and helped pull her down beside him. She tried to pay attention to the plot, tried to laugh when Glenn laughed, but during intermission she returned in haste to the restroom and pushed to the front of the line.

This time for sure! Nothing, except that she had to pee again.

Glenn realized after intermission how subdued Margie had seemed. She said she was fine. *If she's fine, why does she keep heading for the restroom? It must be her time of the month*, he thought sagely. Until tonight he had never even guessed when she was having her period, although it was easy enough to tell when Joyce did. He ought to be more sensitive, he decided.

"Do you have cramps?" he whispered, as they left the theater. He did not even know if she got cramps, now that he remembered Archie had said some girls were spared that part of the monthly torture.

Her hazel eyes flew wide. "No!" she exclaimed, adding bitterly, "but don't I wish!"

That made no sense to Glenn. He had hoped for a romantic stroll through the park on the way home. He had calculated that by the time they transferred buses, it would be getting dark enough for a productive dalliance, but now things did not seem to be headed in that direction.

If only Pop had let me take the car, he thought when they climbed onto the bus. *If only Archie would sell me that truck he's been working on, I could repair it better than he could.* He helped Margie up the steps and dropped some nickels into the cashbox.

By the time they captured a place in the back of the bus and it pulled out onto State Street, he saw that she was trembling. "What's wrong?"

She pressed her lips together, trying not to cry. Irene had predicted that Glenn would question whether the baby was his, which had made Margie upset. "He'll know it's his! If there is one, that is," she had said.

"That's what boys do," Helen had chimed in. "You might as well keep quiet. Just let Creep's friend take care of it before you get any bigger. No sense in losing a steady boyfriend."

"I wouldn't let Creep's friend within ten feet of me," Margie had huffed. She could not imagine such a mortifying scenario.

"What is it?" Glenn pressed. "You're unhappy about something." A pause, then he solicitously murmured that he hadn't understood her answer to his question about cramps. "Did I do something—do I smell bad? Do you want to walk through the park?"

"My period is late," she muttered.

He still didn't infer her meaning. "Oh good, well it ought to be dark—"

"No, Glenn!" she whispered. "It's *three weeks late*. Plus, I've got morning sickness and—oh, all kinds of weird things going on."

"You mean—"

"I mean you may as well know." She watched the color sink from Glenn's face and wondered if her girlfriends might be right. Was she that naive? It wasn't fair that *boys* never had to worry about periods or cramps or morning sickness or having to drop out of school or anything like that. Maybe he thought she was trying to trick him.

She took his hand and was surprised how cold and dry it felt. "When I first started throwing up, I thought it was just nerves or flu or something, but …"

Glenn shook his head as if stunned.

Why didn't he say something?

The bus stopped at Seventh South so a negro family could get off. It took a minute for the family, jostling packages, to descend the back stairs. Then the bus lurched forward and continued on for what seemed like an eternity before stopping at Ninth South, where several elderly women wobbled down the aisle toward the front door. Glenn still remained silent. The bus pulled away from the curb. Two teenaged boys three seats ahead kept turning around to stare, then mutter, then guffaw.

Margie couldn't stand it. *How could they know anything? I was whispering!*

"Please say something, Glenn."

More silence. He shook his head helplessly.

Suddenly Margie thought she was going to be sick. Why had they chosen the back seat where the fumes were the worst?

She started to stand while the bus was still moving. Glenn pulled her down to the seat.

She swallowed and yawned to ease her nausea and glanced at Glenn, who still looked as ashen as she felt. *Well good grief, he isn't going to lose his figure or endure any horrible pain or*— Then she thought of his church-going family. In that respect, she had it easier than he would.

She tried again. "Creep said he knew someone who could help me get rid of the problem," she squeaked, her throat tightening.

No one was pulling the buzzer, so the bus picked up speed. Another minute went by, then Glenn reached for the cord. When the bus stopped, he helped Margie toward the steps as if she were in need of his assistance.

She stepped down and leaned against the stairwell, looking up at him. "Do you hate me?"

He almost managed a smile.

Relieved, she stepped out into the humid night.

He jumped to the curb and shook himself like a dog emerging from a pond. "I'm sorry, Margie. I can't think of what to say."

Say *something!*

"Um, how do you feel … about the situation, I mean."

"I try to pretend it's not real," she said, "but it is." She looked down at her body and sighed ruefully. "It's like an alien power from Mars has taken me over. Seriously, that's how I feel."

"How long? I mean …"

"I've been waiting and watching for a few weeks now. I haven't been able to believe it's true. I even *prayed*. I promised God I'd be better, but it didn't help. Then my mother yelled at me and told Creep what happened," her voice cracked.

He took her hand and they began walking. "Wait, what am

I thinking? We should have transferred so you don't have to walk." He checked his pockets for change.

"No, I'd rather walk. Really."

"You're sure? Me too, actually, if you don't mind."

"Glenn, even though I truly didn't want this to happen," she said through tears, "if there is a baby, I don't want to kill it." This was the first time she had called it a baby, even to herself, and the word sounded odd.

"Then that's our first decision."

By the time they reached Sixth East, the summer monsoon had hustled a rainstorm that spit water at them. They walked faster, holding hands, neither of them having thought to bring an umbrella. Nobody in Utah ever did.

Glenn told his parents the news in their bedroom on Sunday after church. His voice broke as he apologized for disappointing them. "We didn't mean for this to happen."

His parents exchanged a long look, and his mother bit her lips and blinked back tears. Glenn knew he wouldn't be able to stand it if she started to cry. His girlfriend's tears had worn him out the night before.

At last his father said, "Sit down, son."

Glenn sank down opposite his mother on the bed and his father leaned against the door. There was a long silence.

"You've had a little more time to think about this than we have," Evan said.

"Just since last night, actually."

"Well, that's a few hours more than the few minutes we've had. How do you suggest we resolve this?" He came to sit beside Rose and took her hand.

Glenn's words caught in his throat again. "I … I have to find a better job, and that's the main thing. Then I can support her and the baby."

"If you're sure that this is …" Rose began, her voice shaking and then fading off. "I mean, is Margie sure?"

Glenn shrugged. "She says she is, that she has, um, you know, missed once, almost twice. She says she has morning sickness and other things I don't know about."

"Well, let's assume for the moment that she's pregnant," Evan said. "If you both think so, then it's more than likely the case. Margie is still in high school, isn't she?"

"She's going to be in her senior year. She turns eighteen in December. Once I find a better job, we can rent an apartment."

"Glenn," Rose said softly, "do you realize the baby will be coming by March? Right around then, anyway. It's almost August."

"You need to marry this girl," Evan said.

"Well, even a studio apartment would be all right."

Rose shook her head. "You'll need a kitchen when the baby comes."

"A lot of folks manage with less," Evan said. "On the other hand, sometimes their infants die too. I don't think we want our family living out of a cardboard box." Evan reached for his notebook. "It seems to me, we need to make a list and put things in the right order. You would be working full time *now* if you could, I suppose."

Glenn nodded. "Of course. If I'm married I can get a job with more hours," he said.

"Let's hope so," Evan said, wishing Glenn already had a degree. "First off, the marriage, and you need to go job hunting immediately. We'll talk to the bishop, that is, if Margie and her mother don't mind."

"Her mother doesn't go to church, I don't think." Glenn felt miserable.

Rose sighed. Her own pious parents had long preached that a couple should not even kiss until they had exchanged vows in the temple (not that she and Evan had followed that kind of advice).

"You need to talk to the bishop too, Glenn. You officiated the sacrament today. You shouldn't be doing that if you're not square with the church."

Glenn cringed. He had always hated those little talks with the bishop. *What does my private business have to do with him, anyway? Margie will pitch a fit if the bishop scolds her.*

His father was still talking. "Next, you need a place to live, and it needs a kitchen."

"We can't live with her mother," Glenn muttered. "The duplex is too small, and Darlene has gone berserk. I guess she's forgotten she had Margie before she turned sixteen." He bit his lip, realizing that what he said made Margie sound cheap. This was giving him a headache.

"All right, deciding where to live is number two. Is Margie working?"

"No. She tried to check at the market, but they didn't have any times open. Lately she's been kind of sick, like I said."

"So you need to extend your work hours, and maybe Margie can work part-time, at least for a while. After we talk with Margie and Darlene and the bishop, we'll figure out the practical side. Nothing will happen tomorrow, not with the celebration of Covered Wagon Days, so let's accomplish what we can today."

Glenn nodded. Somehow he had never pictured his adult life quite like this, with Pop still in charge. At least no one was raving like Margie's mother. They adjourned to the living room to make the agreed-upon telephone calls.

nine

Annabel skittered up the stairs to her room with energy that belied the temperature, the heat rising half a degree with every step. Her sisters were sprawled in their underwear on the double bed near the window.

"Mama, Papa, and Glenn all left," Annabel announced, "after they took turns making phone calls."

"Who did they call?" Bethany asked lazily. "Where did they go?"

"They talked to Margie and someone else, maybe her mother, and then the bishop."

"Why?" Carolee wondered. "We were at church half the day. What's going on?"

"I figured out this much. There's going to be a wedding!"

"Whose wedding? Who would get married in this heat?"

"Glenn! Glenn and Margie. We're going to get a sister-in-law! We're going to be sisters-in-laws to Margie, and we're just barely eleven!"

Her sisters sat up. "When?" Bethany asked. "Before Christmas?"

"Next Sunday, I think," Annabel said, "at the ward."

"Not in the temple?" Carolee asked.

"No. Maybe that takes a while to arrange. I heard Mama say they should get married on July thirty-first. She sounded like she was trying not to cry, you know?"

"*Mama* said *what?*" Carolee wondered.

Carolee and Bethany grabbed their sundresses and prepared to rush downstairs.

"Don't bother," Annabel said. "They all left, and Joyce is on the telephone with Peggy. She won't let us get anywhere near. She told me not to eavesdrop when that's just what she was doing." Annabel stuck her nose in the air and said, "*I'm* not a child," imitating Joyce.

"Do we get to be flower girls?" Bethany wondered. "I've always wanted to be."

"I think we're too old," Annabel said.

"*I'm* not a child!" Carolee reiterated. "We're probably too young to be bridesmaids."

"So we won't even get new dresses?" Bethany asked.

"Does Joyce get to be a bridesmaid?" Annabel demanded. "Why is Mama upset? If they don't want Glenn to get married, why don't they just say no? They never have trouble telling *us* what to do."

"How could Mama make us all new dresses by next Sunday?" Carolee said. "We'll probably just have to wear our Easter dresses." Her eyes lit up. "Let's switch them around and confuse everyone at the wedding."

"That's fine for you two," Bethany said, then she held up a finger and they all listened.

"The front door," Carolee announced. They dressed and tried not to race downstairs. In the kitchen Glenn was rustling up canned soup and crackers for a late supper.

"Your eyes are bugging out," he muttered. "Make yourselves useful and set the table."

"You aren't the boss of us," Annabel spat back. He aimed a swat at her, while Carolee went to the buffet for a tablecloth. While they gathered the dishes, they began humming "Here Comes the Bride" until their parents emerged from their bedroom, at which Bethany swiftly changed the tune to "Come, Come Ye Saints."

Over a supper that began in silence, their father announced that "Margie is going to be moving in after she and Glenn get married on Sunday. We all need to do our best to make her feel welcome, so we need to plan." He gave the triplets a stern look.

One by one they shrugged—innocent, for once. "Joyce has a double bed," Bethany began sweetly, "or Margie could sleep on the couch."

Her father turned away. "She and your brother will be living here for a while so he can attend classes, work, and save money," he said. "Glenn, you'll need to switch beds with Joyce. Joyce, you're going to have to sleep in the single bed for now."

Joyce gasped and threw down her napkin. "How come Glenn sins, and I get punished?"

At the mention of sin, the triplets' eyes widened and Glenn turned scarlet. He kept his gaze on his soup spoon. This had to be the most humiliating day of his life. *Sure, it could be worse. I could get caned like in China—or Darlene might shoot me. The bishop could excommunicate me.*

The bishop had just put them on probation, saying their marriage signified a first step in recognizing the gravity of their wrongdoing. Everyone in the ward would be counting on their fingers once the baby was born and would soon know they had jumped the gun. *If only we could move away!* Glenn thought.

Still, it had been amusing that Darlene had acted as meek as a bunny even when the bishop intimated that this was all her daughter's fault for not having set limits. Margie had not been impressed by that. For a minute Glenn thought she might tell the bishop Glenn had planned it out and had even brought his bedroll when he came to see her, or that she might storm out of the bishop's office and refuse to cooperate. If she rejected the church, Glenn would be caught in a homemade war.

He snapped to when he saw his father's hand pat Joyce's. "You are not being punished, Joyce. You're helping. But if you ever find *yourself* in this situation," his voice grew stern, "you will *not* be getting married. You will sit at home and wait for your boyfriend to get out of jail. We'll charge him with statutory rape."

"Evan!" Rose warned from the other end of the table, as the triplets sparked with questions.

Glenn took a breath. *Is that what Pop thinks? That I belong in jail?*

"What's—?" Carolee began, but her father overrode her.

"You're a good girl, Joyce, and you're going to get a new room as fast as Glenn and I can fix one for you on the west side of the attic away from the stairs. That will give you a window and some privacy. Your sisters aren't riding tricycles up there anymore, so they can start cleaning and sorting and making room. We're *all* going to be making adjustments, so we might as well begin with good hearts."

Glenn took a breath. Maybe his father didn't despise him—earlier he'd thought Pop might remember how it had felt to be nineteen. Probably his father was just looking out for Joyce, counteracting Glenn's bad example. But Glenn wasn't so sure Pop wouldn't make good on his promise and shoot anyone who touched his girls.

Somehow, making love with Margie had not felt like anything that had been discussed today. Not one moment had felt
like he had committed some heinous sin. *Well, afterward maybe
he felt guilty.*

But now this. How would he and Margie possibly make
love with his sisters right above their room and his parents on
the other side of the bathroom? He sighed heavily. *Maybe Pop
will let us take the car sometimes.*

Rose cleared her throat. "Girls, during the week, we need
to bake brownies and cookies for the reception on Sunday. I
told Margie's mother we would help out. There will only be the
two families present, along with a few church people."

Clearly, supper was over. Bethany and Annabel began to
clear the table, surreptitiously observing as their parents rose
and embraced for a long minute. Glenn and Joyce headed for
their rooms. Carolee murmured under her breath, "Statue—
statue-story—" and slipped toward the living room to locate
the big dictionary.

⚷

Hugo Stuka returned to Princess Alice's barn well after
midnight as the full moon transformed a thousand leaves to
silver. As far as anyone knew, Salt Lake City had hired an elephant trainer, not a *mahout*, but in truth he was both. Princess
Alice remembered far more from her past than her perfor-
mances in the circus. She remembered being wild. Tomorrow
the grounds would be packed with people celebrating Covered
Wagon Days, so Hugo wanted Princess feeling content.

She greeted him with a low rumble, as if to say *let's go*. He
threw a blanket over her upper shoulders and added a harness.
Once they were out in the yard, he stood before her and

tapped her trunk. "Lift up, Princess." She placed him deftly on her shoulders. He positioned his knees between her ears and gripped the harness. "Move up, Princess!"

Her trunk waving to analyze scents, Princess strode out to the unpaved circle. She moved silently even when Hugo allowed her to lope. Their huge combined shadow circled the park in the moonlight, finally pulling up at Liberty Lake. The sleeping ducks and geese peeked under their wings, squawked, and flapped indignantly over to the island.

Hugo dismounted and praised the elephant, then together they waded into the cool water. Princess sighed and squealed as she rolled her huge body, creating waves and churning mud. Using her rolled blanket like a sponge, Hugo methodically washed the elephant, pressing into every fold and crease.

Once she was clean, he leaned back against her side. For an hour or more, they watched tree silhouettes caper against the moon. Hugo thought about their long journey together, traveling the length and breadth of the country and sharing the decades. He felt sure that the princess remembered all of that too.

When clouds obscured the moon, the pair waded to shore and Hugo gathered the tools of his trade. "Move up, Princess," he said softly. She walked beside him back to her barn to spend what remained of the night.

⚷

Despite Glenn's current troubles, Joyce truly believed she could talk her way out of anything. The secret, she felt, was establishing lines of trust before they were tested, rather than remaining reticent like Glenn. For instance, during slow bits of her shift, she confided to Lois, her supervisor, tidbits from her last school year and then from her family life. At home, she told her mother about Lois, about Sybil on the third floor, about Lenny, the wise-cracking, overweight man in Luggage, and about Dorothy, who ran the Tiffin Room. Unfortunately, Mama did not seem inclined to discuss the new and fascinating topic of Glenn and Margie, not even when Joyce remarked that she looked forward to Margie moving in, which was perhaps a tug on the truth.

The chance that Margie might become a real friend did not compensate for Joyce having to move upstairs, even though her makeshift closet space would be expanded. Only plaid drapes separated her new bedroom from her little sisters. Deep down, she was furious with Glenn, disdainful of Margie, and upset with her parents. Nor was she pleased to have to be on the upper floor at all. However, she realized that the general disarray had prevented anyone from noticing her stash of new clothes, which was lucky. She decided to keep her deepest feelings to herself for now and found that her mood improved as she gradually unloaded the doubled-up hangers and got everything organized.

She didn't mind helping her mother with baking for the wedding reception; in fact, Joyce liked creating anything fancy. She had noticed that Mama was not emphasizing cooking skills anymore the way she had with Joyce and that she barely managed the household. It was fine for Joyce, since she saw to most of her own needs, but the Terrible Trio weren't getting an education in domestic skills. Joyce found it useful to have been taught to sew beginning when she was nine. She received compliments on the clothes she made. She had hoped to buy her own sewing machine with her summer earnings, although now she could see it was impractical to think about that for the moment. She and Mama would continue sewing and baking together, though, omitting such topics as Glenn and Margie, sex in general, stealing in specific, and especially Harvey Pratt. Joyce hadn't mentioned a word about Harvey to her mother.

Mr. Men's Wear is what they all called Harvey Pratt, the young man with the long dark lashes and turquoise eyes, as well as a slippery smile that looked sexy and spiritual at the same time. With his wholesome look, he had the ability to shift from piously sincere to insouciant in a moment, without any effort. Sybil had told Joyce how last winter Harvey fractured an ankle sledding and every sales girl in the store had seemed ready to help carry items about in Men's Wear for him. Maybe they became accustomed to his use of crutches, for they still did his bidding, from what Joyce could see.

Nevertheless, she too had a fierce crush on him and suspected he knew it. He lingered, smiling lazily, whenever they chatted over the counter. Not only was he a consistent flirt, he knew everything about merchandise, marketing, and store gossip. Through him, Joyce had learned that Wanda, who worked in Infants, had been fired after they searched her upon leaving work for the day.

Harvey was even able to critique women's makeup and offered Joyce tips. One afternoon when she teased him about his long eyelashes, he had suggested she try false ones. "It's really all you need to accentuate your eyes," he had said with a grin.

"Are you a fashion consultant?" she sassed. Later that day, she slipped over to Cosmetics, where Connie pulled out a tray of false eyelashes for her to consider.

"You'll have to trim them to fit," explained Connie, holding up a magnifying mirror. "But I think you'd look fantastic."

"Maybe," she demurred. "Let me think about it."

When Connie turned to help a customer select a skin cream, Joyce edged a pair of dark brown lashes into her left hand and scooped the other little packages into a pile. The telephone behind the counter rang. Joyce flashed a helpful smile at Connie, then stepped over to intercept the call. By the time she hung up, a tiny bottle of cosmetic glue had joined the eyelashes in her pocket. She kept both hands visible as she swept up the remaining lashes and put them away.

That night she showed the pair to her sisters. "They don't look real," Annabel complained. The triplets watched as she trimmed and shaped the eyelashes with a pair of nail scissors. Carefully she glued one to her eyelid, then blinked seductively. Her sisters burst into applause.

She first wore her false eyelashes on a routine date one Saturday with Albert Storey, who lived in her ward. He took her to a Charlie Chaplin film and Snelgrove's Ice Cream Parlor on South Temple. She didn't really like Albert that much, but everyone at work had chatted about the film. This was her chance to see it. He teased her as they ate ice cream, suggesting that if she wasn't careful one of her eyelashes was going to fall into the sundae.

So much for them looking natural! After the date, she trimmed the lashes again, varying the lengths of separate hairs, tapering them off at the ends.

Sunday morning before church, she thought her mother offered more than her usual scrutiny, but Rose didn't comment. Gratefully, her mind, like everyone else's, was on the wedding ceremony and the reception planned for that evening.

When Joyce saw Albert officiating behind the sacrament table, she sent him a virtuous smile, thinking it helped to have a boyfriend handy during the long summer months. Even a boy as dull and blunt as Albert could be useful. But after the meeting, Albert stood behind her in the aisle, waiting to leave the chapel, and laughed while whispering "fake lashes."

Joyce tossed her head, refusing to reply. She tried to edge forward, but it was no use because so many worshipers had squeezed into the aisle from the back pews. Albert moved closer, bending so that his mouth nearly grazed her ear. His breath enveloped her face with the smell of sinus.

"Are you Minnie Mouse?" he whispered.

Furious, Joyce decided to get even. "Oh, Albert." She half turned, smiled sweetly at the waiting ward members, then stage-whispered, "I'm so sorry you're not feeling well." She fluttered her fingers vaguely toward her nose, tapping her index finger between her eyes.

A pause. "I'm fine," he panicked. "I mean, I'm not sick, not with the flu, I just ..."

Joyce pretended to be confused as she surveyed the tightly packed congregants. "Oh good. Well, you know, with your breath, I thought you might have one of those sinus head-aches." She came to an empty pew, sidestepped along it, and squeezed out the chapel door. She was not desperate enough to let Albert denigrate her!

Once she gained the sidewalk, she noticed three girls her age in a group fall silent at her approach. She smiled brightly, as if she didn't know they had been talking about her brother. "I have to hurry home," she called to them. "Sorry I can't chat." As she walked away, she made a mental note that each of those catty creatures deserved a snub. She would choose her moments.

By five-thirty they were all back at the ward helping Darlene arrange refreshments. Since Margie didn't have any bridesmaids, Joyce announced that she would see if she might need help getting ready. She found her in the restroom looking back over the shoulder of her pale yellow suit.

"Does my slip show?" Margie asked anxiously. "This suit is lined, but I put on a slip just in case."

"Not at all," Joyce lied, spotting a bit of lace along Margie's calves. "Can I help with anything?"

"I just want to find a quiet corner to wait for the bishop. I can't take the ammonia smell in here."

Joyce led her to the coat racks and searched for a neutral topic of conversation. "So, what's the date today? The thirtieth?"

"July thirty-first. Does that sound like a good day for an anniversary?"

"Perfect, because Christmas and Valentine's Day are on the other side of the calendar. You have a better chance at getting an anniversary present."

Margie smiled. "Good thinking."

"You might have to educate my brother about such things, though."

"You're right," Margie giggled. "When we reached our six-month anniversary after going steady, he didn't even notice."

Joyce started to bring up high school, then remembered Margie wouldn't be going back. Finally she asked, "Did you get your things moved in all right?"

Margie shrugged and said, "I think so. The closet is small," she observed. "I mean, mine at home is too, it's just that there are two of us now. We squeezed my trunk in beside Glenn's bureau, and I stacked a few boxes in the other room." She preferred not to mention that she really didn't have too much more to move, compared to Joyce, who always seemed to have the perfect outfit for every occasion. She knew Joyce didn't have to add a scarf or sweater to make an outfit look different.

132 The Flynns owned a piano too, something Margie had always wanted to learn to play.

"Fortunately, your room is below mine, so you won't hear the Terrible Trio thundering around. They make an unbelievable racket."

Margie giggled again, then saw her mother waving from the opposite hall. "I guess it's time to get started." Impulsively she reached for Joyce's hand.

"Don't tell me you're nervous!" Joyce whispered, noticing how cold Margie's hand was.

"I guess I am a little. I've never gotten married before."

Joyce accompanied her down the hall, but then Margie, looking pale, ducked into the restroom. "Tell them I'll be just a jiffy."

During the brief ceremony, the bishop urged them to become worthy to seal their marriage in the temple the following year.

"As if this one doesn't count," Joyce heard Darlene whisper.

As if I would ever settle for a tiny wedding like this! Joyce thought. She had helped procure the family gift, a handsome radio for the newlyweds' bedroom. There were few people and few gifts, and the ceremony was short. Fifteen minutes into the wedding, the couple, having promised fidelity, was allowed to kiss. Glenn enveloped Margie in a lasting embrace.

AUGUST

ten

To Joyce's disappointment, Margie proved to be a less-than-gregarious sister-in-law. She slept late in the mornings and then was often sick. By the time Margie wanted to be social, Joyce was on her way to work. When Joyce had time at home, she found Margie preferred to keep to her bedroom, listening to the radio and flipping through magazines rather than encouraging Joyce's plans to cook, create clothing ensembles, and chat.

Thus Joyce was doubly excited when Mr. Men's Wear invited her to join him on break in the Tiffin Room. She was not entirely surprised. During her shifts for the last week or so, Harvey had seemed to pop up everywhere. He would even fall into step as Joyce walked down a store aisle and observe her over the heads of customers.

He likes me too, she blissfully told herself all week. *He really likes me too.*

She ordered a 7 Up. He insisted she split one of the Tiffin Room's renowned cinnamon rolls, which turned out to be a ploy, she soon concluded, so he could dip one corner of his linen napkin in his glass of water and then dab the stickiness from her fingertips.

Did he pull this little trick with every female? Never mind, she decided. A radiance grew within her as she watched him speak. She was so entranced, she entirely lost what his thread of conversation was about a management seminar he had attended last week.

"It's a huge problem," he was saying as she tuned back in. He still held the fingertips of her right hand. Did he feel the thrill coursing from her fingertips deep into her body? Maybe, for he gazed intently at her from his shining azure eyes.

"A huge problem," he repeated intently.

"How huge?" *Where in the world was this going?*

"Oh, employee theft is an enormous problem," he said with a smile that suddenly appeared sly. "You know, some employees rob their departments blind."

Joyce felt her throat close. He *couldn't* know, could he? Not about *her*. She blinked furiously with the eyelashes he had encouraged her to obtain. There she sat with her stolen lashes, her stolen Barely Red lipstick, which was smeared slightly now on her linen napkin. He let go of her hand, crumpled his napkin, and tossed it onto the table.

"But then," he said, "maybe not *everyone* has noticed that you have sticky fingers, Joyce."

Despite a *thunk* in her chest, she smiled and fluttered her lashes. "My fingers are clean and sweet now, thanks to you, kind sir. Not sticky in the least."

He stood and dropped six bits on the table.

He couldn't possibly know! I've been so careful.

Conscientiously, Joyce refrained from stealing for days, merely setting aside a few items that could be returned to stock if some question arose. Whatever Harvey's game might be, she would beat it! Meanwhile, Harvey continued to flirt, and she flirted back.

Maybe he just wanted my attention. Surely he will soon ask me out for a date.

He did—precisely when her virtue faltered and she decided she could not resist a pink lace camisole displayed on a mannequin. As usual, she took several varieties of sizes and colors into the dressing room. As she expected, the pink model felt good, utterly feminine but invisible under her prim navy shirtwaist dress. She folded her old brassiere and stuck it in her underpants, then returned a cluster of camisoles to the shelf. She felt so stunning that she was hardly surprised when Harvey came and stood close behind her as she signed her time sheets.

"We should go out sometime," he said in a low voice.

"Maybe so," Joyce said. She added a little shrug to appear almost indifferent, then turned to face him.

"Are you free this weekend—say Saturday night?" he said.

She pretended to consider. Not for the world would she admit to having to ask permission. "I think so. I'll check."

"Good. I'll give you a call."

Strangely enough, he didn't ask for her telephone number. Oh well, he could look it up in the directory. He had asked her out on a date! Surely he would follow through.

Friday evening passed, second by second, as she waited for Harvey's call. Meanwhile, Joyce did her best to ignore her mother's obvious efforts to nurture Margie, who after all was practically a mother herself. Saturday afternoon Glenn and Margie claimed the family car and disappeared. Joyce lined her chest of drawers with fresh paper and sorted her underwear. Out went anything torn or over-stretched. The pink camisole shimmered on top of the pile.

She wore it Sunday under her lavender sheath dress, which she had daringly walked out of the store in, concealed beneath her raincoat on a fortuitously stormy afternoon. She contemplated Margie, seated by Glenn in the alcove. *What did it feel like to no longer be a virgin?* She rinsed her camisole that evening to keep it fresh for the next occasion, washed her hands, and left the bathroom to a pale Margie. Of all the inconveniences her brother's wedding had brought, sharing a bathroom with yet another person (or two) was not one Joyce had considered until it happened. Still, she refused to be glum.

She imagined wearing her pink camisole on her first date with Harvey. Perhaps a bodice button might unintentionally come undone and show the merest blush of pink lace. Or if she wore a sleeveless blouse, it might show a pink strap dropping down her shoulder. Such possibilities to reveal a hint of skin or underwear would multiply with the other boys her age once school began, but she might never see Harvey again, she realized.

We just have to go out before the summer ends!

Home life had grown even more complicated. At first, she had pictured herself heroically befriending Margie in the face of Glenn's longstanding resentment, easing the pain of her parents' silent grief and the triplets' bewilderment; but in fact, now she felt more concerned about holding center stage. Why was it that her parents doted on Margie as if she were an orphan and not a sinner? The triplets already had a big sister, yet they hung onto Margie's every word at dinner. They begged her to play board games. Maybe they thought Margie would faint from sorrow while Glenn worked his shifts! Or maybe they did it deliberately to rankle Joyce.

In her opinion, eleven wasn't such an innocent age. She had done some bad things when she was only eleven, though of course, she had allowed no one to find out. But really, it hadn't been her fault when a classmate named Cory had yanked up

her gathered skirt at recess so everyone in the general vicinity
could see her underwear. As she walked home, she had noticed
him riding up and down Browning Avenue on his bicycle.
She cut through the alley and found a long stick, then stooped
behind a hedge to wait for him. When he rode by, she jammed
the stick into his spokes and ducked back. Cory screamed, his
voice mixing with the screech of his brakes and the crash of the
bicycle. Joyce shivered, not having expected so much noise.

Terrified, she whispered a swift prayer to Heavenly Father
for protection. She hadn't meant to hurt that nasty boy, not
that much, at least. Joyce kicked the broken stick aside and
rushed to Cory's aid. She knelt down opposite the driver of a
car who had squealed to a halt and was looking very concerned.
Blood streamed from Cory's nose. Quickly his wrists began to
swell. His sobs became interspersed with screams, as he realized he had lost the use of his hands for now.

"Looks like you went over the handlebars and caught yourself coming down," the driver surmised sympathetically. "Well,
at least your head is in one piece."

Cory's mother was summoned. Taking in the downed
bicycle, the car in the street, and her bloody son, she enfolded
him and wept. "You might have been killed!" she kept exclaim-
ing. The growing group of neighbors murmured assent.

Joyce nodded along with them, impressed that her simple
sabotage had been so effective. When the witness agreed that
the car had not been at fault in Cory's mishap, that it must
have been a loose stone, the driver left. Cory was taken to the
hospital for x-rays. For the remainder of the school year, he
was hampered by the weight of casts on both arms. He steered
clear of Joyce and shot her sharp looks in class, but without
ever lodging an explicit accusation. Joyce's modesty was thereby

defended and she honored this auspicious justice by never telling anyone what she had done, not even Peggy, who thought herself privy to Joyce's entire life.

For years Joyce had looked forward to turning sixteen, and now that she had, her driving and dating were limited thanks to her brother's misbehavior with Margie. Still, she assured herself, when summer was over and her junior year began, it would be time to shine. No weak-kneed, immoral latecomer to the family, however winsome Margie was, would edge Joyce into the wings.

"I think we should turn this job over to Margie," groused Annabel, as she and Carolee loaded weeds into the small wheelbarrow so Bethany could dispose of them. "It's too much for us and too early in the morning!"

Bethany laughed. "Do you want Margie throwing up all over the garden? That's what she does in the mornings. I even caught her throwing up at church before they got married. I thought we'd all come down with stomach flu."

"But we didn't," Carolee mused. "Maybe it's nerves. Everybody acts nervous around Margie, that's for sure!" She plopped down on the grass at the edge of the garden and brushed the dirt from a ripe tomato. "This is the best part of gardening," she said, biting into the firm red flesh. Her sisters found ripe tomatoes and joined in.

"The worst is canning," Annabel said. "Even worse than weeding. I figure Margie can help Mama and Joyce with that if we do the weeding and picking."

"Speaking of which, I'd better get a basket," Bethany said, "for all the things that are turning ripe."

"I'll get a couple of pails out of the shed," Carolee offered. "Even if *we* can't consume all those raspberries and blueberries by the back porch, someone will. We'd better hurry up before it gets hot."

"I'll get something for the strawberries," Annabel added more cheerfully. "In fact, I'll go tell Mama it's time for shortcakes."

When they reconvened for an official harvest, the conversation resumed. "Do you realize that summer is two-thirds gone?" Carolee mourned. "You two haven't finished your projects, and I think there's at least one other mystery to solve."

Bethany gave her a long look. "Are you thinking what I'm thinking?"

"Wait!" Annabel interjected. "You didn't solve the Frankie Stuart case, Carolee! He's still missing. You just eavesdropped on Papa talking about it to Mama. That doesn't count!"

"Papa knows what happened," Carolee said archly. "So, why shouldn't I get my information from him? And Annabel, I haven't seen you walk into church with Pearlann Jones either. Remember when the bishop asked Brother Droopy-Cheeks to pray for her the other day? What does it mean? Where is she? And Bethy, I bet Princess Alice is going to be moved up to that new zoo before you teach her any new tricks."

"She already knows about thirty," Bethany said, scooting toward the peppers. "Hugo said she remembers every trick she ever learned."

"You aren't even going to try to teach anything, are you?" Carolee challenged.

"Of course, I am. I even have something in mind," she extemporized. *Time to change the subject.* "Let me guess. The new mystery is Glenn and Margie?"

"Yes, it is, and I bet we can think of questions we don't have answers to faster than we can pick vegetables," Carolee challenged, glancing at the house to make sure no one was sitting near an open window. "Why was that wedding so strange, for starters?"

"That's right," Annabel agreed, dropping a cucumber into a pail. "Why was everyone so sad except for us? Even the bishop said we added brightness to the occasion—something like that. At first, I thought he meant because of our Easter dresses."

"Why did they hurry through it?" Bethany put in. "Mama at least could have sewn Margie a wedding dress instead of letting her wear that yellow suit."

Annabel grabbed a separate pail for raspberries. "I heard Darlene tell Mama that Margie should not get married in white anyway. Why *wouldn't* she wear white? What does *that* mean?"

"Why does everyone call her Darlene?" Carolee demanded. "She's Margie's mother, after all, isn't she? I mean, she looks old enough to be her mother."

"That's because she smokes," Bethany said. "Joyce told me she read in a magazine that smoking gives you wrinkles. Papa doesn't like us to call her Darlene."

"But Darlene prefers it," Carolee shot back.

"Why didn't they get married in the temple?" Annabel asked. "All we hear in church is 'Get married in the temple! Get married in the temple!' Then along comes a wedding and it's not in the temple."

"Maybe it's because Darlene smokes," Bethany said solemnly. "Is she even a Mormon?"

"Of course she's a Mormon," Carolee said. "She has a bishop, doesn't she? Margie is a Mormon. Who do we know who isn't a Mormon?"

"Lots of people," Bethany said. "Plenty of kids at school aren't Mormons and neither is Hugo. He told me he has a glass of wine with his dinner at night but never at work because the smell of alcohol makes Princess Alice mad."

"Bobby's mother next door told me she might go to church if she didn't have to give them ten percent of her money. What with the Depression, she said, she can't afford to be a Mormon," Annabel added.

The sisters shared a moment of sympathy. They each dutifully set aside a penny from each dime they earned, but they still secretly resented it.

"You know," Carolee said, "You should tell Bobby's mother that the church is giving away groceries to poor people. It's called welfare. Anyway, we're off the subject. Who has another mystery question?"

Bethany said, "Here's my main question. Why is Margie living with us? Aren't married people supposed to live in their own house?"

"Lots of people live with relatives these days," Carolee replied. "It's because of the Depression. Nobody seems real happy about it. I know I'm not. We've got Joyce parading through our room at night to get to her room."

"She's mad she doesn't have her old bed and no wall between our rooms, just drapes," Annabel sighed. "I think Glenn and Margie must be really crowded, even though they got the double bed. They make so much noise down there." She tapped squashes together. "Boom-ba, boom-ba, boom! That's even with Glenn's radio on."

"Why do they go to bed so early," Carolee sniffed, "when no one tells them to? I'll bet they could stay up until midnight if they wanted. I know I would! Why don't *they* stay up?"

"Well, the thing I hate is leaving Joyce's old room vacant," Annabel said. "All it has in it are storage boxes. I asked Mama why Joyce can't sleep there instead of crowding us, and she just said it wouldn't work in the long run. Does that mean they'll be there forever?"

"Who knows?" Carolee sighed. "We-e-l-l-l," she said, her voice dropping mysteriously, "I looked up that word Papa was talking about. I finally found it. It's called statutory rape."

"What does it mean?" Bethany whispered, feeling a hum between her eyes as if she were about to bump her head. "What did you find out?"

"The dictionary doesn't have much," Carolee shrugged, "just that it means sexual *inter-cross* with a minor. I didn't know what that means, so I looked up the words. It doesn't mean a *miner* like the seven dwarves. It means someone under twenty-one."

"What does the other part mean?" Annabel asked.

"Sexual *inter-cross* had about four other words in the defini-tion I didn't know," Carolee said, "and none of them made sense. That's the trouble with dictionaries. You just get in deeper."

"Well, *sexual* must mean something about having babies," Bethany said. "Papa told me the father plants a seed that grows into a baby."

"A *seed*?" Annabel hooted, pointing at the garden. "Do you think the baby's ripe yet? Who wants to pick a ripe baby?"

"Stop it," Bethany said, not about to get silly. "Babies grow inside the mother, right? It's the seed planting part I don't get."

"I figure the father just hands over the seed to the mother and she plants it," Carolee said, "maybe through her navel. Before I could look up any more words, Papa came in. But first I saw one word having to do with pee. I think it might be like you said, Bethy, when it comes to peeing in the canyon." She lowered her voice to spell, "P-e-e-n-i-s."

They exchanged uncomfortable glances. "I think it's that part that goes with the octopus glands," Bethany said. "Everyone has to pee, though. In fact, Margie pees fifty times a day." She fell silent.

Finally Annabel stood and brushed dirt from her knees and hands. "I don't know what's going on with Glenn and Margie," she said, her voice trembling, "but I know Mama and Papa would *never* do anything nasty with a seed, or pee, or—" Her voice broke off at the end.

"I think," Bethany said slowly, still thinking of the bedroom left empty, "that we should watch for any signs of a baby."

eleven

Margie heard the triplets' voices outside and went to the kitchen to find something to eat. She felt hungry all the time except for when she was getting sick, but she couldn't stand the smell of food cooking, especially meat. She sliced a loaf of homemade bread and hunted for jam. Hopefully this would stay down. Glenn had ruined some ice cream for her the evening before by bringing her a dish of strawberry ice cream that was partly melted. Now she probably wouldn't be able to eat ice cream until Easter. She couldn't imagine living with the Flynns until Easter! It was horrible being with people she hardly knew, especially when she felt so awful all the time.

For one thing, she couldn't help with cooking, so she and Glenn always ended up doing the dishes. When Glenn worked, Margie washed them herself and let them dry in the drainer. That's what Darlene had always done. Rose never said anything, but Margie knew her mother-in-law preferred the dishes to be dried one at a time with a cloth. *Why did it matter?* That was the thing about Rose. She didn't boss Margie around, but she was the kind of person who made you feel you ought to be doing something useful, even if you felt rotten and you just wanted to lie down. Margie couldn't ever figure out what her mother-in-law wanted. At least with Darlene, everything was out in the open. Before they married, she had envied Glenn having a mother like Rose, but now she wanted her own mom back. She missed her house. She missed her bedroom. She even missed the tiny bathroom she had only had to share with Darlene. Eight people sharing a bathroom ought to be illegal!

At least, Margie hoped, throwing up all the time meant she wouldn't get fat. She was determined not to let her body change too much. No one needed to even know she was pregnant until the end, and then they could say the baby had come a little early. Joyce let her know she knew what was going on, but Margie refused to confirm it. Really there was little she could discuss with Joyce. She didn't feel right talking to her about boys when she was married to Joyce's brother, she wouldn't talk about the baby, and she couldn't talk about high school since it appeared she wouldn't be returning to school. She certainly didn't trust Joyce enough to share confidences with her about the family, not to mention her thoughts about Glenn.

It was her mother's fault she had to live with the Flynns. If Glenn had moved in with Margie and Darlene, it would have been much easier. He had his shifts at the gas station, but otherwise they could have spent all their time together while Darlene was still at work. They could have gone out in the evenings when Creep came by. The house was small, true, but the Flynns' house wasn't much larger, and it was so full of people that Margie felt she couldn't even think, especially since someone was always playing the piano as loudly as Joyce was right now.

Margie had tried going home after her mother left for work and taking Glenn with her when he wasn't working. One of the neighbors must have tattled because her mother came home early one day and demanded Margie's key. Glenn was mortified, even though they were dressed and just chatting. Margie didn't understand how Darlene could stay so mad at her! How was it possible for a human being to remain so perpetually mean?

They really had no privacy at all until his whole family went to sleep. Even then, who knew if someone might at any moment decide to traipse into the bathroom, which shared a wall with the bedroom? The whole bunch of them were forever talking, thumping up and down the stairs, slamming doors, snoring, and joking about things she didn't understand. Even the air in the house had probably been breathed several times before Margie took it in. No wonder her stomach was upset. She was so exhausted, it made her bones ache. If ever she felt like a whole person again, she vowed, she was going to find a job. No, she couldn't, she just remembered, because she would have her baby to take care of. She had never been around a baby, and soon she would have one of her own!

Rose entered the kitchen, saw the loaf of bread on the counter, and said after she wrapped it in waxed paper, "I'm sorry, do you want another piece, Margie?"

"No, this is all. I was just going to wrap the bread."

Rose smiled as if she actually believed her and tucked the loaf into the breadbox. There was never a girl who needed more mothering than Margie, Rose thought. "Would you like to walk to the market with me and get a little fresh air?" she asked.

"Um, I don't know. I'm just so tired today. Or do you need someone to help you carry groceries?"

"No, I just thought you might want to get out of the house."

"I would, but—" She shrugged and laughed a little. "I don't want you to have to carry *me* back home."

"Tell you what, let's go right now and take the car. Evan doesn't need to go to the police station yet. Since everything is ripening, we don't need much right now, just a couple of cuts from the butcher."

At the thought of a meat counter, Margie had to look desperately out the window, hoping she wouldn't gag. "Maybe I'd better not," she managed.

"Whoops, I said the wrong thing, didn't I? Well, I'll just go. Is there anything you need or anything that sounds especially good to eat?"

"Maybe some more soda crackers and honey. Honey usually tastes good, especially on your homemade bread."

"I have some dough rising now," Rose said. "I'll be back in a few minutes."

The piano music had stopped. "Mama, wait. You could ask if *I* want to go!" Joyce said while she stalked into the kitchen. "Let *me* drive. No one has time anymore to go driving with *me*." She looked pointedly at Margie, who flushed.

"All right, Joyce, as long as you're ready right now. We need to get back so Papa can go to work."

In a few minutes, Margie had the house to herself. She could hear the triplets' voices rocketing through the screened windows from the backyard. She wandered through the rooms and wondered if she could have a bubble bath in peace, but no, Evan would want to shave before work. She could walk over to the gas station to see Glenn, but she really was tired. A thought struck her. Now was her chance to get a good look at Joyce's closet.

Upstairs in the make-shift bedroom, she had gotten a peek at the immense wardrobe when she realized she was trapped. The triplets had dashed in the back door and were running up the stairs. With nowhere to go, she hastily moved so she was standing inside Joyce's door when the girls reached their room.

"Hi," Margie said, stepping into their room. "I thought maybe I kicked off my sandals in Joyce's room, but I guess not. What have you been up to?"

"We picked a ton of berries and vegetables," Annabel said, plopping down on her bed, heedless of her dirty hands and knees. "They practically filled up the kitchen counter."

"That's good. Maybe I should start washing them. When your mother gets home, I'll see whether she plans to can them or wants them in the refrigerator."

She hurried down the stairs. Sure enough, grimy pails clustered in and around the sink. Margie took a deep breath, pulled a pail of raspberries out of the sink, and started picking through them. She popped one in her mouth. It was warm from the sun but nonetheless tasted good. She ate another and hunted for a colander in the cupboard.

Rinsing and sorting, she thought about Joyce's clothes. It occurred to her that a part-time job wouldn't generate enough pay to be able to accumulate so many outfits, even with an employee discount. How did Joyce do it?

Margie could think of only one way, yet it didn't seem likely. She would ask Glenn about it. He probably wouldn't know or care. Margie considered herself skilled at getting people to confide in her, though. She decided she would find out.

⚷

At dawn that Wednesday, a sturdy wooden trailer-truck with a logo reading Hogle Zoo backed close into the elephant barn at Liberty Park. The driver lowered the tailgate into a short ramp, which he braced from below. Hugo shoveled grapefruits, potatoes, and bananas into the front of the trailer bed and padded the rest of the bed with hay. Meanwhile, the driver, animal trainers, city commissioners, and a small contingent of press collected in a cautious half circle.

It was a little before Princess's usual breakfast time when Hugo unlocked the barn. He could tell from the squeals and rumbles that the elephant knew something was up. Carefully, murmuring and stroking, he secured her harness and attached a short chain. He unlocked the rear chain, tapped her left front leg with the bull hook, and gently turned her toward the doors. She raised her trunk suspiciously, sorting the scents of strangers, but headed out willingly enough.

"Move up, Princess," Hugo said when they reached the ramp onto the trailer. He tapped her left front knee again. "Move up!"

The elephant tossed her head at the gathering but sedately walked up the ramp. Hugo attached her chain to a link on the trailer's side. He stroked Princess's ear and whispered praise, for clearly she knew what this meant. He edged himself back to grip the trailer rim and tossed the first grapefruit into the princess's mouth. Camera lights flashed and someone cheered.

For a second, Princess Alice froze, then swung her head toward the onlookers. Hugo caught the sudden glare from her left eye. In an instant Princess threw back her head, shot forward her trunk, and roared, jerking violently upward and snapping the chain. Before Hugo could begin to calm her, she had butted and kicked the offending trailer to splinters. Planks and fruit flew over the cowering humans.

Hugo soared from the disintegrating trailer, striking his head as he crumpled a few feet from the tire. Princess Alice whirled toward him. "No!" someone screamed. "It will stomp him into the ground!"

Princess roared again and crashed down the ramp. Then she paused to sniff at Hugo before stepping carefully away from him. Indignation emanated from the elephant as she returned to her barn and was chained in a hurry by another zoo keeper. In a few minutes, she trumpeted for breakfast.

Hugo was stirring by then, but the mayor and parks commissioner insisted he remain still until the wailing ambulance pulled to a stop. He was taken to the hospital and diagnosed with a minor concussion, then released. After telephoning his wife, he returned to the zoo to check on Princess Alice. She gave him a light but reproving whack with her trunk as a reminder that a determined blow from her could kill him, then they proceeded calmly with her bath.

The shock and momentary terror of the morning's incident resonated in the afternoon newspaper under the headline, ELEPHANT INJURES 1, WRECKS TRAILER. Hugo's injury was characterized as an attack, and the elephant's refusal to relocate was described as an attempted escape. No explanation was given for how an escaping elephant might have been captured and subdued when her trainer lay on the ground injured. Unfortunately, the reporter reached the manager at the Sells-Floto Circus, who took belated revenge by intimating that he had sold Princess because she was a potential man killer.

Even the president of the Salt Lake Zoological Society called for her destruction. "We could maintain two Indian elephants for the cost of feeding one dangerous animal of this type," he said, erroneously suggesting that Princess Alice was an African elephant and less manageable than her Asian cousins.

A public meeting was called for Friday morning to discuss

the elephant's fate. The Flynn family prepared to attend. The day before, Joyce and Margie collaborated on a petition for the younger girls to march door-to-door south of the park. Friday morning, bedecked in the sailor dresses Rose had finished at midnight, the triplets turned heads as they strode with Evan in his dress uniform up the crowded steps of the City and County Building. The rest of the family walked behind. Proudly, Bethany added their sheaf of signed petitions to the stack that had already accumulated on the mayor's desk.

In response to remarks by the mayor, commissioners, and Zoological Society president, Hugo stepped forward and mounted the speaking platform. He, too, wore a uniform and had replaced his cap after the flag ceremony to cover the bandage above his right temple.

"Please let me tell you about Princess Alice," he began the speech he had practiced carefully for days. "She has been my friend for forty years. Princess is an Asian elephant from India. She is intelligent and friendly. True, she is large, but any elephant who lives long enough will grow to her size if fed adequately. She is the only elephant, maybe, in America to have produced four calves, and Salt Lake City should be proud to own her.

"The princess is around crowds of people all day but has never intentionally hurt anyone, not here and not when she was in the circus. What she doesn't like is being hauled around in a truck. Also, cameras scare her. The other day, she was frightened. She wasn't trying to harm anyone or escape. As for the idea of buying two new elephants," Hugo feigned confusion, "has this Depression ended and nobody told me?"

The crowd laughed, then cheered.

"We'll try again," the mayor promised at the meeting's end. "If Sells-Floto sold us a man-killer, they certainly didn't mention

that. The next time we move Princess Alice, we'll get a veterinar-
ian and a stronger trailer. We invite all of you to come and see
her perform once she's settled into the beautiful new zoo!"

Satisfied, the Flynn family left, along with the dispersing
crowd. The triplets had expected this result. The evening before,
they had requested, and Bethany had led, a kneeling family
prayer on Princess's behalf. Bethany had added a silent personal
plea: *Let her stay in Liberty Park. Let her stay near me. Let her
always be my elephant.*

twelve

Later, considering the alternative, Joyce was glad Harvey had made his threats over a soft drink in the employees' cafeteria on Saturday afternoon. He could have blindsided her on the date they'd made for that evening. She couldn't believe at first that a young man with such a sweet smile could be so crass and calculating, but he made it clear he was.

"Let me be direct, Joyce," he said, keeping his voice low but his eyes fixed on hers. Joyce nervously nibbled on ice as Harvey said, "I know about your hiding place for stolen goods on the shelf next to the top one in the employee dressing room. You can clean it out, of course, but my duty might be to interrupt you, maybe with the store detective, and catch you red-handed."

"I don't know what you're talking about," Joyce whispered. An ice cube slid down her throat and she coughed.

"Don't talk, darlin', or I'll head straight to the dressing room and just tip your bag upside down in front of the detective." He paused to appreciate the flush rising in her face. "Or I could have a talk with your bishop."

I knew I was right to mistrust that whole priesthood business,

Joyce thought. *Men always stick together. What sympathy could I expect from a bishop who blamed only Margie for getting pregnant?*

She forced herself not to panic or cry. "Why are you *doing* this, Harvey? Why are you accusing me like this and asking me on a date at the same time? I don't understand."

"Why shouldn't I ask you out? In the long run, I bet both of us end up having fun. There's a new Al Jolson movie for starters."

Joyce shook her head hard, then remembered not to let a false eyelash flip off. "Listen, Harvey, I just made a mistake— okay, a *couple* of mistakes. I'll put everything—I mean both things—that I took by mistake back on the racks."

He merely gazed at her.

"You've taught me quite a lesson," she hurriedly added. "Believe me, I'll never try it again."

He took a long sip of cola. "Doesn't matter how much you took, Joyce. You're a confessed thief now. What's more, you're *my* thief."

What did he mean by that? Is it possible things could get even worse? No, he was full of bluster and could not prove anything. She began to say as much, but his gaze had turned cold and she decided not to press him for what evidence he had. She drew a long breath. "What, exactly, do you want?"

Now his eyes grew playful again.

How does he do that? She took a relieved breath; this wasn't so bad after all.

He grabbed a spoon and held it beneath his nose like a villain's moustache. "Your job or your body," he growled and then laughed. "A little summer excitement for me, Joyce; for you, perhaps something you won't learn in high school."

Joyce tried what she hoped was an arch look. "My job or my body. Well, let me think it over," she said playfully. She let her eyes linger on his, then looked down demurely. "I *really* need my job. Besides, Lois isn't in today, so I can't do anything drastic."

His grin widened. "Understood."

She had heard stories about what couples sometimes sneaked off and did, but she didn't see how Harvey could deprive her of her virginity on a date. Was it even anatomically possible to do that in a car or theater? "However," she added smoothly, "I'm such a *good* girl that I can't possibly give you an answer now. Let me at least have time to think."

He lowered his glossy head. "Fair enough. I'll give you an hour, then I'll pick you up outside the employee exit at, say, fifteen after five. Maybe we could drive through the canyon before the movie. If you're such a *good* girl, you should let your mother know you won't be home until later."

He kissed his forefinger and touched it to her nose, then swung out of the booth. "Must get back to work now." He dropped change on the table, smirked at Joyce, and walked out.

Although the taste now sickened her, Joyce sipped watery root beer for a minute. Scheme after scheme whirled through her mind. This wasn't a problem she could take to Peggy or to Sybil upstairs. Or to her parents. Not to anyone, really. Not even to God.

Even if she covered her tracks and never stole again at work, Harvey might find a way to expose her. At the very least, he could start rumors. Also, he seemed to be headed for a job in management. No doubt, he could make working here unpleasant and possibly bar her from working in any other department store. It was so unfair, now that she was trained!

On the other hand, she considered herself quite good at kissing despite her limited experience. If she let him kiss her tonight, maybe even a lot, would he expect more later? Even if he didn't, a hundred kisses wouldn't remove his threat. He could tell on her whenever he wanted. And what if he called the police? Papa would hear about it and then so would Mama. She simply couldn't bear facing them. She clutched her handkerchief, determined not to cry.

Deep breaths. Okay, how did she need this to turn out? How could she take the upper hand? She didn't want to date Harvey. There was nothing attractive about him anymore. He was an evil schemer and she was his latest prey. She *had* to fix things today. Tomorrow she could take the sacrament and receive another week's clean slate.

First, she needed to free herself from Harvey's threats, from exposure at work, and from having to give in to whatever he considered romance. *How to get there?* Ideas flew at a rapid pace. Some of them winged past, others settled and she placed them in order, then checked for any weaknesses. With her confidence returned, she even smiled at the waitress as she stood to leave the cafeteria.

Joyce kept a brisk pace and went directly to the employee dressing room, which was empty (thank goodness), and made sure her bag was undisturbed. She moved it to a more obscure position. Next, she climbed the back stairs to Personnel, hoping she might look as wan as she felt.

She sat down with the assistant manager to explain that a family emergency required her to leave that evening on a train for San Francisco; she didn't know how long she would have to remain there. She apologized for not having been able to give two weeks' notice. Of course, she assured them, she did not expect them to save her position. They had already been so good to her and she probably wouldn't be back before school started. She requested a sheet of letterhead to write an apology for Lois, folded it, and handed it back to the assistant manager, assuming he would probably read it before placing it in an envelope. After she was assured that someone from Notions would be able to watch Lingerie for the last hour of the day, she went downstairs, picked up the telephone in the employee dressing room, and called her friend Peggy.

"I need a favor, Peg. Call someone and stay on the line for at least fifteen minutes. I'll give you a divine blue scarf if you do this little thing for me and never, ever tell it to anyone, okay?"

She knew from trying to reach Peggy in the early evening that Sister Pratt, Harvey's mother, shared her friend's party line. With Peggy on the line, Harvey could not call his mother. Joyce also knew Sister Pratt's garrulous neighbor across the street. She liked to waylay Joyce in the market and press her to the edge of endurance by discussing an upcoming visit to Idaho or other family matters.

Placing Myrtle firmly in her mind, Joyce dialed the number for Men's Wear. As usual, Harvey answered.

"Hello," she bleated, trying to make her voice sound old. "Is this Harvey Pratt? The Harvey Pratt who lives on Kensington Avenue? Yes? … Well, Harvey, this is Myrtle Bligh from across the street. I hate to bother you at work, but your mother is running—no, roller skating—up and down the street. What's worse, she's only wearing a little robe or something. Well, maybe a nightie."

Joyce choked back a giggle as Harvey exclaimed that she must be mistaken.

"No, I'm sure it's her, Harvey. I just thought I should let you know before some busybody calls the police. She's speeding past again. Oh dear! I have to go."

She replaced the receiver, grabbed her bag, and walked

swiftly to the bus stop, waiting there with an eye toward the area where Harvey usually parked. Standing behind a large man, she peeked around when Harvey, his brow furrowed, stomped toward his car. Joyce tried to blend in with the other people at the bus stop even though she didn't think Harvey was paying any attention.

Getting even always feels so good. Especially getting away with it! No job, no date. Best of all, no proof of wrongdoing. Added up, that meant no threat.

Trembling slightly and lacking the patience to wait for either the Fifth East or Seventh East bus, Joyce boarded the State Street bus and requested a transfer. She found a window seat halfway down the aisle and pressed her cheek against the warm pane. She was sure she had escaped unscathed because no one had even checked her bag on the way out. She had left before Harvey could raise an alert, preoccupied as he was with his mother's odd behavior.

She knew that when Harvey arrived home and found that all was well, and then discovered that Joyce had quit her job, he would put it all together quickly enough. But who cared? He couldn't prove her a thief to anyone at ZCMI. He wouldn't dare tell her father anything when he had tried to blackmail her. He could hardly tell her bishop—or his—that he knew she was stealing but hadn't told anyone or even that someone had said his mother was roller skating barely clad. Sister Pratt would be furious that her son had come home from work to check up on her! Joyce gave herself a tiny hug. *This was the perfect crime.*

Really, she had played it right, she thought. Maybe she should have ditched the brocade underwear and pale gold scarf coiled in the bottom of her bag with the price tags still on, but why? A full week had passed since she had set those items aside. She would tell her parents she had resigned because the before-school rush was wearing her out or that a male supervisor had made her feel uncomfortable with his advances—nothing specific enough, though, to prompt Papa to investigate the immoral, over-confident rogue who thought he could play her and get away with it.

A shadow fell across her knees and she glanced up. A rangy boy with blond hair, one she realized she had seen before on the bus, smiled down at her. Surprised, she smiled back and moved her bag. He took the aisle seat, his shoulder and knee still protruding a bit into the aisle.

"I hope I'm not crowding you," he said easily. "My shoulders are more of an asset on a football field than on a bus."

She laughed easily. He didn't look old enough to be playing for the University of Utah. "South High?" she asked.

"No, Granite. Do you go to South?" She nodded. "I'm David Anderson. Actually, I'm running for student body president this fall. I wish you could vote for me."

"I do too." As the bus bumped along, she ran his good looks and his poised introduction through her mental catalog. *Just as spoiled by girls—or maybe by his mother—as Harvey.* Still, the doting seemed to have turned him into a confident teen instead of a sly and calculating cad. She glanced at him and noticed his expectant look. "Oh, sorry. I'm Joyce Flynn. It's just my junior year this fall."

He smiled again. "I've seen you on the bus before, Joyce. You don't ride too much farther, do you?"

"Just a couple more stops." She repositioned her bag on her knees.

"So, maybe I'll see you next week? On the bus, I mean."

"Yes. Or—no. I have so much going on right now. I quit

my job today, and that will throw off my whole routine. I probably won't be taking this bus again."

"I see." He eyed her gravely. "Too bad you quit. I guess now I'll just have to ask for your telephone number."

As he spoke, the bus lurched to the curb along Thirteenth South. She had to transfer or walk a mile. "We're in the phone book," she said as he stood to let her out. "Flynn on Sherman Avenue."

She had to run for her next bus, but once aboard, she felt relieved by the good omens. She had escaped Harvey's snare, caught her connecting bus, and met a football player running for student body president at Granite High. Maybe he would call or not. The important thing was that her treasure was safe at home and her secret about how she had gotten it was buried in the past. If Harvey could not bring it to light, who could? She would look forward to her last paycheck in the mail and two free weeks without having to work, during which she could coordinate her wardrobe. She might do a little more shopping too. *How convenient that no one knows me at Auerbach's department store,* she thought.

Evan liked to tell rookies in the police department that detecting might seem inexplicable on the surface. "It's not exactly intuition," he would say. "It's really experience—long experience, and logic."

It was that experience that lay below his decision to ease his unmarked car to the curb when he saw Rodney Johnston, Pearlann's make-believe groom, walking north on Seventh East. Rodney had been interviewed after Pearlann disappeared. He had denied any awareness of her whereabouts and seemed too dim to lie effectively to police officers. Nevertheless, Evan decided to follow his hunch.

"Hop in, Rodney, I'll give you a ride."

Rodney stuck his head in the passenger window. "I didn't do nothin'," he protested.

"Come on. It's hot. I'll give you a ride." Rodney climbed in as Evan turned down the dispatch radio. "Where are you headed, Rodney?"

"I don't know. It sure is hot."

"Sure is." They continued north in silence for a few minutes. "Hey, Rodney, have you been to American Fork lately?"

"No, I don't like it there. The training school is stupid."

"Stupid, huh? Well, I asked because I thought maybe you might have seen a friend of mine. You know Pearlann Jones, don't you?"

Rodney shook his head no, but in a moment his right leg began to jiggle.

"You don't know Pearlann? I thought she was your friend."

Rodney shook his head no again. His hand crept toward the door handle.

Evan sped up, made it through a yellow light, and unobtrusively set the master door lock. "I haven't seen Pearlann in quite a while, Rodney. Have you seen her?"

"Well, I *did* see her," Rodney mumbled.

"You *did* see her. That's good. That's a load off my mind." Silence.

"By the way, when was it that you saw her, Rodney? I'd like to say hello."

"I don't know. Anyway, she got mad."

"Pearlann got mad at you? How about that. It sure is hot today. Are you hot?" He reached inside his suit coat for his handkerchief and handed it over. "Do you want to wipe the sweat off your face?"

Rodney buried his face in the cloth and began rubbing. While the young man was doing this, Evan reached over and patted his arm. "Gosh, why would Pearlann get mad at you, Rodney?" Evan turned left onto South Temple and headed for downtown.

Rodney squeezed the handkerchief into a rope. "I don't know. She just didn't want to, … to … You know." He made a gesture with his fingers.

"Oh, I see. You wanted to have sex and she got mad?"

"She did it *once* but not too good. Just one time. Then she wouldn't do it again and got mad."

"How about that?" Evan waited behind a few cars for the traffic light to change. "When Pearlann got mad at you, did you get mad back?"

Rodney sighed deeply.

Evan waited, then finally remarked, "Hmmm, imagine her getting so mad at a good friend like you. My gosh, where were you when all this happened?"

A pause. "We were by a wall. You know that little wall in the park?"

"I don't know if I'm thinking of the same park you're talking about, Rodney. How did you get there?"

A pause. "We rode the bus," Rodney said, his voice lifting as he remembered. "Pearlann said there was a little place with a roof"—he shaped his hands like a gazebo—"by the wall where she said we could get married. Then, she said, it would be okay if we did sex all we wanted." His face clouded over. "But it only happened once …"

Evan turned onto Main, heading north, then turned east again at North Temple. "So, you were headed in this direction?"

"We rode one of the buses downtown and walked to the little wall."

Evan felt the hairs on the back of his neck rise. "Maybe you mean the canyon. Did you go to Memory Grove?"

Rodney said nothing. He mopped his face again.

"Tell me this: when Pearlann got so mad at you, Rodney, did you get mad too?"

"I guess I did. I got *so* mad at her!"

Evan turned left toward the mouth of City Creek Canyon. "What happened after that?"

"I got so mad, I put my hands around her neck like this—" He cupped his broad hands in front of him and shook them. The handkerchief dropped to the floor.

"I see, Rodney. This is important. Did you leave Pearlann in the canyon afterward? Can you show me where you left her?"

"I can show you," Rodney said. "I bet I can remember where she is."

"That's good, Rodney. That's real good." Evan turned up the radio and called for back-up.

thirteen

Carolee was the first to see their father's photograph on the front page of the local section. When she and her sisters gathered to read the article, they felt pride in their father, but horror at the details of his discovery.

"I feel terrible for Brother and Sister Jones," Annabel said.

Reading behind them, Rose wiped away tears. "Maybe now her family can find a little peace and not always fret about it or hope she'll be found," she said. "I think the only thing worse than having a child die would be not knowing where she was."

The girls nodded gravely. Annabel lowered her voice after Rose left the room and said conspiratorially, "Now we know where Pearlann is, so my summer project is finished. Carolee, you don't know where Frankie Stuart is yet. You heard what Papa suspects, but Frankie *could* come whistling down the sidewalk tomorrow and you wouldn't know anything about it."

"At least I gathered some information on my own," Carolee huffed.

"I'm still the first one finished because Pearlann has been found," Annabel protested. "Frankie is still missing, and now so is Mary Agnes. Looks to me like you're going backward, Carolee. And Bethany hasn't even started."

Bethany admired the photograph of their father in the newspaper. He wore a hat with his summer suit and posed with a shovel. "Well, Annabel, when did *you* begin to investigate?" she asked mildly. "When you saw tonight's paper?"

Annabel's chin jutted out. "I'm still first to finish."

"Fine," said Carolee. "You help Mama peel peaches while Bethy and I work on our projects."

Annabel scowled. Peeling peaches in the summer heat was the worst task. It meant having juice trickle down your arms and getting your feet stuck to the floor. "Nice try, but the peaches aren't ripe and, when they are, you know everyone has to help. Maybe even Margie this year."

"Where is she?" Bethany asked. "Let's show her Papa's picture."

"And Joyce," Carolee added. They knew their older sister would be livid when she found out they'd gotten to the newspaper first.

They found Joyce and Margie together in the backyard, outside at the edge of the garden. Clouds rumbled and the air felt damp. Margie held a basket in her hand. Joyce tugged at its handle. "I told Mama *I* would do this," Joyce said crossly. "Now give me the basket before it rains."

"She asked *me* to pick snap peas," Margie said. "I don't mind. I like seeing how things grow in the summer."

"*You're* growing this summer," Joyce smirked. Margie reddened.

"Has either of you seen today's newspaper?" Carolee intervened. "Papa's picture is in it because he found Pearlann. Look, he's right on the front page."

"Doesn't he look handsome?" Bethany put in.

"He sure does," Margie agreed, looking over Bethany's shoulder but keeping both hands on the basket.

"Oh, *you* just think he looks like Glenn," Joyce said, snatching the newspaper away.

"What?" Margie asked.

"I've seen you flirting with Papa, just like you act sweet to Mama. It doesn't matter. Girls," she said in a voice that clearly included Margie, "while I read this article, please finish your picking so Mama and I can make dinner." Joyce flounced over to the swing, flipping the newspaper straight.

Wordless, Margie knelt beside the garden. Homesickness swept over her. But Darlene had started being nasty to her too, she reminded herself, especially since Margie's stomach began poking out. Anyway, Margie didn't *flirt* with Glenn's father. She admired his good looks and sense of authority and secretly hoped Glenn would grow up to be like him. She rubbed her tears away by pretending to wipe her sweaty brow on her shoulder. "It's so sticky today," she murmured, and picked faster.

Bethany stooped beside her. "Joyce is just plain mean sometimes," she whispered. "We don't think you're bad."

Margie tried for a smile and sniffed. "You know what? It looks like more raspberries are ripe."

"We'll handle those," Carolee said. "They'll be good on ice cream. Grab a basket, Annabel."

Picking hurriedly as the clouds lowered and gusts of wind lifted their hair, the triplets scarcely noticed when Joyce dropped the folded newspaper on the back porch. Suddenly a hard blast of water from the garden hose drenched Margie and the triplets.

"That should cool you down," Joyce said sweetly, turning off the tap and picking up the newspaper to stalk into the house. The others, stunned and dripping, stared after her.

"Feels good!" Carolee yelled toward the screen door. "Thank you very much."

"These are my only clean shorts," Margie said, shaking water out of her hair. "My blouse is soaked. I'm drenched to the skin."

"I'm going to tell Mama," Annabel said, handing the basket of raspberries to Carolee.

"No," Margie said, "please don't. I don't want more trouble. I'll just change before Glenn comes home." She stood. "Can you girls finish up?"

"Sure thing," said Bethany. "We're almost done anyway."

A crack of lightning flared and thunder crashed a few seconds later. "Get away from the big tree," Carolee yelled. A deluge chased them; frantically, they grabbed and clutched the garden plunder and ran into the house.

"We better not get polio because of Joyce," Annabel muttered.

***

The rain crashed inches above Sol's head as he placed Frankie at one end of the cot and rousted Mary Agnes from the other. The little girl woke up wailing, as Frankie slept on.

"Come on," Sol exclaimed. "It's time you had some exercise." He swung through the trap door and helped Mary Agnes through. "Jeepers, what a storm! Aren't you glad I brought your jump rope inside?"

Mary Agnes slid onto a wooden kitchen chair and cautiously shook her muddled head. Seeing she was still at Sol's house, she began to whimper.

"Now stop that sniveling. I'm fixing you some crackers and milk. Then you can jump for a while, okay?"

Suddenly Mary Agnes felt hungry, starved, but she also had to go pee about a gallon. Grabbing a cracker, she hurried away and closed the bathroom door firmly behind her. Sol whistled as he set out jam and dill pickles. *That girl smells a little strange today. Time for a bath,* he thought.

Mary Agnes ate but she whined between bites. "Where's my mother? Why am I still over here?"

"You have only been here a little while, you dummy bunny."

"No, I—I slept here." She thought she remembered waking up on the cot and finding herself in the same kitchen over and over again. How many times had she played jacks on the linoleum floor? Her memory seemed like watercolors dripped into liquid.

"Have a pickle. Yes, you stayed overnight, Mary Agnes. Remember? A few days later, you stayed over again. Of course, you went home in between, silly. Maybe you're going loony!" He stuck his thumbs in his ears, wiggled his fingers, and extended his tongue. "Bl-e-e-a-a-g-h-h!" The girl didn't even smile.

Sol grabbed the jump rope. "Okay, grouchy-puss. I bet I can jump rope better than you. Want a contest?"

"I want to go home!" She looked longingly at the back door, which was latched too high for her to reach. The front door was locked, too. Where did Sol keep the key?

"Okay, you can go home," Sol shrugged. "And you don't even have to walk. Your mother is going to pick you up on her way back from the store."

"How do you know, you big fibber!"

Sol made his lip tremble. "Now you've hurt my feelings. She just called! Didn't you hear the phone ring while you were in the bathroom? Maybe you were peeing too loud."

Mary Agnes thought about that. Her headache was easing, and her mother was on the way. Suddenly she felt cheerful. "My mother really is coming? You promise?"

"Double-X, Mary Agnes." He crossed his arms on his chest in a ridiculous way. "Now there's a smile from my best girl. Just one thing now. Your ma asked me to make sure you were nice and clean before she picked you up. Why don't you jump rope for a few minutes while I run a big bubble bath?"

"No, I can have a bath tonight at home."

"Okay—except your mother wants you clean. To be honest, you don't smell so good, Mary Agnes. It's your hair, I think. Then there's the surprise for you." He gasped and clapped a hand over his mouth and said, "Whoops."

"What was that?"

"I wasn't supposed to say anything about the surprise."

"What surprise do you mean?"

Sol kept his hand on his mouth and widened his eyes, shaking his head helplessly.

Mary Agnes stared at him suspiciously. "I did see some pink stuff on the edge of the tub," she murmured.

"The bath salts. Well, a princess bath this one time. Bubble bath and bath salts and foamy shampoo. Start your jump rope, girl, and I'll get it all ready."

He would soak her clothes in the sink while she bathed and find a shirt for her to wear. Then he would slide a sliver of laudanum into a chocolate drop. That would be his wee reward to her for not fussing as he helped her wash everywhere and shampooed her hair.

As her days lengthened, Joyce found her family even more annoying than usual. At first she had dressed up and gone downtown, ostensibly to seek another position, even though a job for a few weeks would be improbable. Mostly she window shopped. She ducked into stores and stole small items until she visited Auerbach's and found she was being trailed by a store detective, which made her wonder if Harvey Pratt had circulated her description around town. Dispirited, she rode the bus home and deposited a scarf and purse in a drawer without even bothering to remove the tags.

One afternoon she fell onto her narrow bed to take a mental inventory of her losses. She could no longer view Harvey as a romantic interest. That was too bad. *Even though he was a self-righteous cad.* Still, she missed the fuss of dolling up for him, flirting with him, and even daydreaming about him. Since she had offended Albert after only a single date, going out with him was no longer an option. She could apologize, but why bother? He wasn't fun anyway. She would meet plenty of boys when school started after Labor Day. On the other hand, the intervening days and weeks were going to stretch into a long boring interim. David Anderson had not called. He probably knew too many cute girls already who were willing to work on his campaign.

On top of that, she no longer had an employee discount or access to the sales floor at ZCMI, let alone the thrill of pocketing merchandise. At least they had plenty of fabric on hand at home, so she could create an outfit or two if she wanted to. Cheered by that thought, Joyce scurried down the narrow stairs so quickly that she nearly tripped. *A person could get killed on those stairs!*

She had been shoved into the attic like Cinderella waiting to be rescued, and it wasn't fair, but she wasn't going to think about it. Instead, she would measure her waist in front of Margie and let her know it was down to twenty-two inches! Unless Margie had walked to the gas station to see Glenn. *In which case she can annoy Glenn instead of me.*

176

But to her shock, she found Margie sitting at the sewing machine next to Rose, their voices and hands mingled over a piece of printed fabric.

"Oops!" Margie exclaimed, snatching a hand back from the darting needle, through a charming giggle.

Mama is teaching Margie to sew. I can't believe it! Joyce closed her eyes and felt her head spin. It was another loss, for only she and Rose had ever sewed together, just as only Glenn had helped their father with the car. Even the triplets knew not to hang around the sewing room without invitation.

"Oh hi, Joyce," Margie seemed to trill. "Can you believe I'm attempting this? Darlene would faint from shock!"

"Let me know when you're finished," Joyce said. Some instinct kept her voice low. Furiously, she went back upstairs and stared out the window. "Darlene would faint from shock!" she imitated.

Suddenly she foresaw the next insult she could expect. Margie, who called her own mother by her given name, would no doubt start referring to Rose as Mom. She could see it as clear as anything. Margie was going to *steal* Joyce's parents from her. After she produced an adorable, demanding grandson or granddaughter for Evan and Rose, all they would want to do would be to dote on the baby. Joyce knew all about that! With a baby in the house, nothing she did would matter. Meanwhile, Margie—who had dropped out of high school—would stay home and sew.

"I could *kill* her!" Joyce muttered. She sank onto her bed and whispered, thoughtfully this time, "I *could* kill her."

There wasn't much to this mysterious thing called death when you thought about it, she told herself. Thousands of people died in wars. Children were starving during the Depression right in the United States. Yet apparently the world kept spinning and everyone pressed forward. Take Aunt Shirley, for instance, who had died even though everyone had tried their best to save her. A person was alive and then, snap, they were dead.

What a nice thought! With no Margie around, everything would return to normal. School would start, Glenn would meet other girls, the family reputation would survive, and there would be no squalling baby to exhaust or enthrall Joyce's family. She would once again have a chance to shine in her parents' eyes. She could not be detected, though. Accidents happened every day, and she had heard her father say most happened at home. *Well, so be it!* Thinking through the details, she decided she could go to the basement and look through her father's tackle box and tools.

A little later she cheerfully prepared salads to chill for dinner and boiled potatoes for hash browns. By the time Joyce set aside the potatoes to cool, Margie was ineptly practicing a hymn on the piano and Rose was ironing.

"Margie, would you like to see my new issue of *Ingenue*?" she asked sweetly. "I'll be back down in a while, Mama, to help finish up dinner."

"That's fine, dear. I promised to drive the girls to the market in a few minutes, but I'll be back by the time Papa gets a ride home from work."

Joyce accompanied Margie up the stairs, letting her sister-in-law lead the way to the triplets' room, and said, "Make yourself comfy on my bed. I just need to put something away." Then swiftly she knelt and pulled up some fishing line she had tied between the newel posts. She decided a height of about four inches looked perfect. Drawing it tight, it looked ready to go, so she rejoined Margie for a chat about fashion and make-up.

"Oh gosh," Joyce said finally. "I need to slice those boiled potatoes. Take your time, Margie. If Mama doesn't need me, I'll come back up."

Margie smiled sleepily and leaned against the propped-up pillow. Here was the perfect opportunity to get a look at the closet.

Joyce stepped carefully over the top step and hurried down. Humming, she began to slice the first potato and noted that her mother had returned and was calling in Annabel to set the table. She heard her father's voice as he came up the sidewalk. Everything was proceeding perfectly.

Then Margie cried out, "Oh my *Lord!*" so shrilly that Joyce was hit by a sudden lapse in control and dashed down the hallway, expecting to find Margie crumpled at the foot of the stairs. When she wasn't there, Joyce sprinted upstairs, forgetting about the fishing line, and snagged her right ankle. She sprawled full-length forward with such a crash that it knocked her breath free.

By the time she pulled her unbroken limbs into a sitting position, her mother was kneeling to one side and Margie was at the other side. From her father's upraised hand dangled a length of knotted fishing wire.

"I'm fine." Tears stinging her eyes, Joyce brushed away the concerned exclamations. "Bruised maybe. I just tripped."

Evan extended his other hand to Rose to draw her to her feet. Rose's eyes moved from the knotted line in her husband's hand to Joyce, then to Margie.

Instinctively Joyce started to reach for the fishing line but then thought better of it. She inhaled deeply, realizing she had to fix this, like she had fixed the mess with Harvey. "Why in the world did you scream like that?" she asked Margie crossly.

"Did I scream? No, I'm sorry. I just—" Margie drew herself

together. "I was startled," she said. "I've never seen so many
new clothes in one place before, except in a department store.
Of course, you did work at the ZCMI," she said.

A tense silence. The triplets, alerted by the commotion, had
crowded around to better view this drama.

"Don't be ridiculous, Margie," Joyce said coldly. "Everyone
has seen the few things I bought with my employee discount."

"That's enough!" Rose said quickly.

Evan looked closely at the triplets. "Where have you three
been the last few hours?"

"Outside, then at the market," Bethany said. "Annabel came
in to set the table, so we came in too. What's in your hand?"

Evan walked past them into Joyce's room. The drawers and
closet curtain stood open. "Rose," he said.

Rose came in, closely followed by the girls.

"Would everyone please get out of my room?" Joyce
shouted. She softened her voice and held up her forearms pitifully. "Mama, could you help me put some ice on my bruises?"

"Just a minute," Evan said. "Annabel, Bethany, Carolee, go
downstairs and stay put for a while."

One look at their father convinced them a protest was useless.

When they had left, Evan raised the fishing line. "This
appears to have been tied between the newel posts, as if to
trip someone."

Joyce gasped, hopefully on cue. "So *that's* why you
screamed!" she accused Margie. "You *wanted* me to come
running up here and fall. Well, I hope you're satisfied, Margie
Landers Flynn. First you shame our family, then you move in
and take over, then you—"

"I don't know what you mean," Margie choked. "I didn't—I
mean, I would never—" Tears started as she reached a hand

toward Rose. "You've been so kind to me. I don't even know what that string is."

"I believe it's fishing line," Evan said evenly. "People fall down stairs when they trip on it, sometimes fatally."

"Exactly," Joyce said. "I must have avoided it going downstairs a few minutes ago and Margie screamed to make me come back up and trip on it."

Rose sank on to the bed, shaking her head as if caught in a nightmare. She held Evan's eyes a minute.

"Joyce, why *did* you go downstairs?" Evan asked.

"To slice potatoes. But then—"

"And you were going to call me down to dinner," Margie whispered. Instinctively one hand covered her abdomen. She turned so pale that Rose made her sit alongside her on the bed and put her head down.

Evan tucked the fishing line into his shirt pocket. "Joyce, take a seat right there in the doorway. Let's have a look at your wardrobe." He ran a hand along the row of crowded hanging clothes. "Rose, have you seen this—all this merchandise—before?"

"No, I haven't."

"Of course you've seen it. Just let me—"

"Joyce, be quiet. Margie, if you're feeling better, why don't you go downstairs and make sure the little girls practice the piano."

"If you feel up to it, would you finish the hash browns?" Rose asked. "We'll talk in a little while."

Margie sent each of her in-laws a long appealing look and then slipped away.

To Joyce, it seemed an interminable time as her parents examined her closet. Her father went to her bureau and began tossing lingerie and accessories into piles on her bed.

Ignoring her protests, Rose looked through the stacks of clothes, some still bearing the original tags. Joyce longed to squeak and cry like Margie but found she was too outraged to make tears come.

They can't prove anything! she told herself repeatedly. She calculated her chances of storming out of the house. *Mama left the car parked in back. If only—*

Evan drew Rose aside, just outside the doorway, so Joyce could not get past them. "Hide the car keys," he whispered, "and ask Margie to feed herself and the girls. Bring up some shopping bags, grocery bags, whatever we have."

Rose nodded and left.

"Papa, I paid for all this. You have to believe me."

"Joyce, I would prefer that your mother not see you in handcuffs, so I hope you'll cooperate. If you're wearing anything you stole, you need to remove it and put on your own clothes. Your *old* clothes. Or you can wear clothes your supervisor saw you purchase."

Joyce gasped. "Papa, most of this didn't even come from Lingerie, definitely not the clothes on the hangers. How can you do this? Margie tries to kill me, and then you practically call me a liar. And a burglar!"

He pulled out his notebook. "A thief," he corrected. "Tell me the departments and supervisors involved." She did as she was told, trying to maintain a vestige of dignity as her father took notes. He remembered meeting Lois Wheeler and decided to call her first.

"But it doesn't *matter* which departments because I used my discount. It's good in every department!"

"I don't want to hear it. Would you prefer I call in another detective or will you willingly go with me to the police station?"

"I'm your daughter!" she shouted.

Evan felt lightheaded from hunger, fatigue, disappointment, and most of all disbelief. He was glad to see Rose return with the paper bags. "Thanks, dear. Would you please watch Joyce change into her own clothes? Meanwhile, you can start filling these bags by department as much as possible. I need to make some calls, and then I'll come back and help."

Winking away tears, Rose began sorting, watching for tags, familiarity, signs of wear, squelching her innate concern for Joyce. Like Evan, she was too horrified by the volume and value of the items around her to even think of intervening, especially after seeing the frightening length of fishing line in her husband's hand. If Joyce really was capable of running so far amok, she realized, it would take a dramatic response to turn her back onto course.

Evan was relieved to reach Lois at work and to find that she was just as personable as before. "I'll explain this to Sybil in Ladies' Wear and meet you at the police station," she said. "I admit there were rumors about Joyce, but we didn't want to believe it. Harvey Pratt in Men's Wear said he had caught her stealing, but he had no proof and I didn't know what to think."

Evan considered. "Let's avoid saying anything to Mr. Pratt for now, if you wouldn't mind."

"I think that's best too. I'm so sorry, Sergeant Flynn."

"Please," he said, "you're not the one who needs to apologize."

Next he called the station and spoke with Charlie Prescott in Juvenile Violations. "She's smart, Charlie. It's her first time in trouble, but she's stolen a lot of clothes. I want her scared enough to stop."

After Margie put dinner on the table for the triplets, she called Glenn at the gas station. Her voice shook as she told him what had occurred. "I know we need the money from your double shift, but I have to see you. We have to talk. I don't know how long they'll be gone. I can't face Joyce, at least until we—"

"Okay, Margie. I'll leave early. Maybe you should walk over and meet me, then we can go over to your house."

"No, Darlene will be home from work and I'm not sup-posed to leave the little girls. They don't really understand —" Her voice cracked.

A pause. "I'll get there as soon as I can."

Glenn was breathing hard and appeared to have run all the way home. He enfolded Margie. "Have you eaten?"

"I can't. I've been retching even though there's really noth-ing in my stomach. What about you? Did you have dinner?"

"I grabbed a sandwich before you called."

He looked over her head to see three sets of young eyes studying them. "Okay, T-trio, you behave. Margie and I need to talk a minute."

He walked with her to the back yard, sat down on the triplets' swing, and put her on his knee. "Tell me."

"I think we'll break the swing! I bet I weigh a ton."

He looked up at the ropes, which seemed secure. "I bet you don't. Tell me."

When she finished, Glenn had to get up and pace around the yard, he was so angry. "I'll throttle that murderous little … bitch! Unbelievable! What goes through her mind? Who does she think she is?"

"At first, she seemed nice to me. I don't know, maybe

even then she hated me because of having to give up her room. She knows the baby's coming. I didn't tell her, but she knows. She probably thought that if I fell, I'd lose it and everything would be like normal for her again. She wasn't trying to kill me too, was she?"

Glenn thought about it while he marched a couple more turns around the yard. "I don't know. Maybe you're right—maybe she thinks she can make things go back to how they were. I thought she'd like having a baby in the family. On the other hand, she was pretty resentful of the triplets when they were born."

"She'll really hate me now because your parents found everything she's been stealing. You wouldn't believe how much stuff they hauled down to the police station."

Glenn quit pacing and straddled the swing again. Margie sank to the ground, leaning back against the tree to gaze up at him. He seemed older somehow.

"We can't live here any more unless the cops lock her up. What did Pop do? Is she going to jail?"

"I don't think so. She wasn't in handcuffs, but he took the string—the fishing line—with him to the police station."

"It's not going to have fingerprints."

"And then she accused *me* of trying to kill *her*. I don't think your parents believe it. Otherwise, they wouldn't have left me alone with the girls."

"You're right, they wouldn't have." He pecked her on the forehead. "No one could believe that, Margie."

She tried to smile, but her lips trembled. "At least you don't."

"Joyce is sneaky. I don't think we'll be able to close our eyes at night. You won't be able to go up to her room again and feel safe or go driving with her or—" He thought a minute. "How would you feel about living on a farm? It's nearby, and I think it only has one cow and a few chickens by now. It's my grand-parents' place at about Seventeenth South."

"I guess that would be okay. But would they put up with a baby?"

"I don't know, but there's no baby yet. The other thing is, Archie's grandmother used to live there in the basement apartment, and they haven't rented it out since she died. It's been a while." He paused and then added hastily, "She died in the hospital, not in the apartment."

"I remember Archie saying something about it, that it wasn't in great condition. Isn't that right? Even so, could we afford it?"

"We'll figure that out. One way or another, Mrs. Flynn, we're going to get out of this house. Can you start packing while I make some calls?"

"Yes."

He gave her a hand up.

"What will happen to my things?" Joyce wailed.

Charlie Prescott stared at her nonplussed. He thought he saw a shadow move on the opposite side of the two-way mirror and assumed it was Evan turning away in disgust.

After everything that's happened, all she cares about is keeping her stolen clothes?

The women from the department store had left after they identified merchandise from the their departments. Joyce was mortified to be on display before her former superiors and people she had considered friends—people who had now agreed to testify against her.

Charlie had explained the process. They would file charges, there would be a hearing, a Juvenile Court judge would consider the matter, and she would probably serve time at the State Industrial School. For the first time, Joyce looked scared, if not exactly remorseful. When he suggested that he might release her to her parents until the court date, she reached for the bright array of clothing as if to re-pack it and go home. When he stopped her, she let loose her wail.

"First of all, Miss Flynn, this isn't yours. It's evidence in a theft case. It's been identified as stolen. Secondly, maybe I shouldn't release you at all because you don't seem to comprehend the gravity of this."

Apparently she did, because she covered her face and her shoulders shook. But why was she crying? Did she understand or was she mourning her lost goodies? He couldn't tell. There would be rules, he informed her. She would have to be accompanied at all times by one or both parents, even at home. She could not drive, no matter who was in the car. If her parents went to church, she would have to attend with them, but she could go nowhere else without a judge's permission. She could not associate, even in her own home, with anyone who had been in trouble with the law.

He turned her over to Evan and Rose with handshakes and a sigh of relief. Their eyes were redder than their daughter's, Charlie noticed. He wondered what possible transgressions his own grown sons may have committed when they were teenagers and decided it was best if he didn't know.

Once the paperwork had been signed, the Flynns walked out to the car in silence. As Evan pulled into traffic, he glanced at Rose. He checked to make sure all the doors were locked. At a red light, he pulled the fishing line from his pocket.

"We need to talk about this, Joyce. Your sisters were outside at the time, so I assume Margie was your target."

"Is it the baby?" Rose asked. "Did you want Margie to miscarry?"

Joyce shrugged and gazed out the window. "We're going to talk about the baby now, after all this time?"

"Talking about the baby is not the point," Evan said. "Staging an injury, maybe murder, *is* the point. I didn't bring this up with Sergeant Prescott because I wasn't ready for that much hell, but you have to tell us now what your intent was." He pulled up at the next semaphore. "Or do we need to go back and add another item to the sheet Sergeant Prescott is keeping on you?"

Fury rose in Joyce's head. "From now on, every time something happens, I guess you're going to drag me off to the police station, aren't you? I should just run away!"

"Joyce," Rose said gently. "What's wrong with you?"

Her defenses dropped. "I'm tired of having Margie around. I lost my room because of her. I lost my *bed*. Now I've lost my job and all my clothes." She began to cry. When she quieted, Rose handed her a handkerchief.

"You can't hold Margie responsible for your theft," Evan said. "Stealing is how you lost your job, and it's the reason you lost your wardrobe, which wasn't yours to begin with!"

"And you're not the only person who feels cramped and displaced," Rose said.

"Glenn and Margie *deserve* to feel cramped. They're the sinners. I didn't do anything wrong! At church they say you have to pay for your sins."

Letting that desperate confession hang in the air for a moment, Even and Rose exchanged glances again while they rode in silence. Evan turned the car into the alley and said, "Joyce, do you realize that you actually conspired to take a life?—two lives really? There is nothing on earth worse than that. Since you've mentioned the church, I think we've overlooked the fact that we need to let the bishop know about this so you can start your repentance."

"I'm *sorry*, Papa!" Joyce exclaimed, her voice breaking. "Do we have to go through all of this again with the bishop?"

"I think we do." Evan glanced at his watch. "I'll call him first thing in the morning. Why don't you go ahead into the house while your mother and I decide how we're going to manage all of this with your sisters. We'll be inside in a minute."

He parked at the end of the backyard. Joyce flung the door open and flounced into the house. Evan and Rose sat in silence for a minute.

"She'll apologize to Margie," Rose said at last. "I don't think she knew what she was doing."

Evan pulled his wife into his arms, and they held each other for a long minute. "I think the less said to the triplets the better," he said, "but Glenn's going to pitch a fit. I would if someone tried to hurt you."

"Yes," Rose sighed. "But Joyce is still a child. She's only sixteen, you know. Not that Margie's much older—or Glenn. I should think of him as an adult, but I still see him as a little boy."

Evan shook his head. "Keep in mind, I was Glenn's age when we got married, and you were his age when you had a baby." He let his mind drift back for a moment, then returned to the matter at hand. "We have a long evening ahead of us, Rosebud," he said. "Maybe *we're* the ones who should run away from home."

Rose laughed. "Let's do it!"

Hand in hand, they went in to face their children.

fourteen

As darkness fell, Evan and Rose gathered their triplets into the living room. There seemed to be more excitement hovering around them than seemed warranted.

"Joyce has made some mistakes," Evan began, "so she'll be staying home for the rest of the summer unless she goes to church with Mama and me. You know it's wrong to take something that doesn't belong to you, don't you? Even if it's something you think you need?"

Each one nodded earnestly.

"All right then." A pause. "I hope you three saved us some supper."

"I'll fix some eggs and more hash browns if there's not enough," Rose said. "Oh, wait—where's Margie?"

"They left," Annabel said, suspense flashing in her eyes as her sisters chimed in with more information.

"It was because of that string you found, Papa," Bethany explained. "Margie hugged us goodbye and said she'd miss us."

"They took everything they owned," Carolee added.

"How could they leave?" Evan asked. "We had the car."

"Glenn was supposed to be at work until nine," Rose said, then realized Margie must have called him.

"Archie came in an old truck," Carolee said. "They even took their wedding presents and said they were going to Grandpa and Grandma's."

"Margie told us to be careful going down the stairs," Annabel added.

"How long ago was this?" Evan asked, moving toward the telephone.

"Just before Joyce came in. They left a note," Bethany suddenly remembered. Her sisters raced into their parents' bedroom to fetch it.

"I'll read it aloud," Carolee volunteered, but her mother extended a hand for the sealed envelope.

"I can see that you're mystified," Evan said, "but I want you to do us a favor. Please get ready for bed as quietly as you can. Pretend like a giant will grab you if you make any noise or talk to anyone, even to each other."

"Papa!" Annabel exclaimed. "We're not babies."

"We know that," Rose intervened. "Keep your light on and read until we come up to tell you good night. Please."

A general sigh, and then the triplets left the room. "When you come upstairs, will you be sure to tell us about the string?" Carolee called back over her shoulder.

Together Rose and Evan read that Glenn and Margie didn't feel safe. "We can fix up the apartment downstairs from Archie's family," Glenn had written, "and all our work and our painting the walls will count toward rent. Or maybe we'll stay on the farm and help Grandma and Grandpa. I should have thought of this sooner, but everything happened so fast. Thanks for welcoming Margie into the family like you've done and

everything you did to help us." He signed his name "with love."
Margie added her name below.

After reading the note several times, Evan and Rose sat in stunned silence. "Maybe it's for the best," Evan said. "We're going to have our hands full."

"But the baby, Evan. The baby is going to cry and get into things. I want to be sure my folks feel all right about this. I don't like the idea of Joyce getting her way either."

"Joyce is going to have her hands full, too," Evan said. "We'll make sure of that. Maybe having a change would be good for your parents. They miss Shirley so much! Why don't you call your folks while I settle the trio? We can talk over supper."

On his way up the stairs, Evan decided to talk with Joyce first, with the triplets reading in conspicuous silence on their side of the curtain. He rapped on the wall, pushed the curtain open, and found her curled up, still dressed, on her bed. She seemed to have shrunk somehow. He sat down beside her but had no idea what to say, especially with six eager ears on the other side of the curtain. Finally he took her hand.

"She was stealing you," Joyce whispered, her voice high and strained. "You didn't see it, but she wanted you and Mama for herself. I just—" She shook her head and her eyes flooded.

"No one can steal us from you, Joyce, not even when you're grown and married. If you thought that would happen, well, no such luck! You know that Glenn and Margie have moved out?"

She nodded. "The girls told me. I think I'm actually going to miss Margie, especially now that I'm stuck at home."

Evan sighed. "Do you want some supper?"

"Maybe." She tried to laugh but only managed a squeak. "Am I allowed to eat?"

"Stale bread crusts and water, that's all the sergeant said we can give you." He chuckled and added, "Go help Mama while I tell your sisters good-night."

Gazing at his triplets, Evan wished he could send Joyce back to their age. He sat down on the double bed with Annabel and Carolee and motioned for Bethany to join them. "I wish you didn't have to know this," he said when they were all nestled around him, "but I don't see any way around it. Joyce got jealous of Margie, and she tied that piece of fishing line over the stairs to trip her. Instead, Joyce forgot about it and fell when she was running up the stairs. Anyway, it's lucky no one was hurt."

The girls thought about this. "That's not why you took all those bags of stuff to the police station," Carolee guessed.

"No, that's because the clothes didn't belong to Joyce. She took them from the store where she was working, without paying for them. She'll never be able to work in a department store again."

"Did you keep the police from locking her up?" Annabel asked.

"No, that's not up to me. Joyce has to go to court and talk to a judge, and he'll decide her punishment." The girls curled closer. "Joyce will also have to talk to the bishop about this because someone could have been really hurt."

Silence. This was scarier than anything they had conjured.

"Is Margie going to have a baby?" Bethany asked bravely.

Another pause. "Yes, she is."

The girls gasped and clapped their hands in delight. "How long will it take?" Annabel asked. "They have to move back here so we can help."

Evan smiled. "The baby isn't due until March, and that's why we didn't tell you. It's a long time to wait."

"We'll be aunts," Carolee breathed, "on top of being sister-in-laws. All of that before we turn twelve!"

"I think people say '*sisters*-in-law,'" Evan corrected. "Goodnight, Aunt Carolee. Goodnight, Aunt Annabel. Goodnight, Aunt Bethany." He turned off their light but doubted they would fall asleep anytime soon.

☞

Late August blazed and the monsoon added humidity. Rose told the triplets to wash their sweaty hair Thursday before supper instead of waiting until Saturday. Bethany said she would go first. While in the tub, she had an idea. After leaving the box of bubble-bath envelopes out for her sisters, whom she could hear struggling through a piano duet, she went upstairs; the idea continued to grow in her imagination as she rubbed her hair dry as quickly as she could and pulled on a clean play jumper and sandals, then slipped out the back door. Maybe she'd be last to finish her project, she thought, but she'd finish it best of all.

Her sisters hadn't really done anything except to find out what their father knew. *Big deal!* Bethany could have switched her project to finding Mary Agnes, and then let Papa solve that too, but no, she would do like she said and teach Princess Alice a trick, and what a trick it would be!

Joyce's old bicycle stood propped against the back porch, so Bethany swung a leg over it and started peddling, cutting through the alley and turning toward the park.

At about the same time, her father dropped by the Schatz home to pitch an idea to them. He told them about his daughter's trouble with the law and said that, without a previous record, probably the judge would sentence Joyce to community service. That had made Evan think of Lara, who was easily as bright as his eldest daughter and needed help with anything she could not do with her left hand.

Why couldn't Joyce spend a few afternoons a week—once school began—doing whatever Lara couldn't do for herself? The Schatz home was within walking distance, and Joyce could hardly resist being touched by Lara's talent as an artist and her efforts to correspond with her brother in Germany. What a contrast Lara's life was to Joyce's focus on her wardrobe and trying to gain the spotlight.

"She can frame your sketches and help clean your room, whatever you needed," he told Lara. "She could help you write letters too. You would be doing a wonderful service for us if you let her be your assistant in the afternoons and on the weekends. You and your aunt need to decide, of course."

Amelia had questions. Evan explained the details of Joyce's situation painfully and succinctly. "This is the first time she's been in trouble, but it's a whopper, I know. I want her to learn from her mistakes, and it would do Joyce a great deal of good to know someone of Lara's character and talent. This would be under your supervision, of course."

Amelia thought about it. "You don't think she would steal from us, do you? We don't have a great deal we could afford to lose."

"No, I don't believe she would ever steal from an individual. She's gotten it into her head that stores have so much on hand, they don't miss it if some of it disappears. Aside from that misguided thinking, she's a good girl and kind at heart."

Evan decided not to mention the fishing line but he hoped that at some point Joyce would imagine what it would be like for Margie to be confined to a wheelchair, if she had fallen down the stairs, and understand the significance of it.

Lara wrote on her sketch pad, "Yes, I would like to try this. 195 Maybe we will become friends."

"I think that's likely," Evan said. "She'll probably introduce you to some other young people your age." He winced inwardly at the loneliness that shone in the girl's eyes.

Amelia saw it too. "All right, let's try it. But tell her there will be no funny business."

"Oh, the judge will let her know that, and I'll reiterate it. If there's any trouble, she'll be emptying bedpans for the old folks around the corner," he said, indicating the general direction of a care center for seniors.

He thanked them, resisting an impulse to pull Lara in for a hug. This worst of cases might conclude well, after all, he decided on his way back to the car.

⊶

Ignoring the few other zoo visitors, Bethany stood directly in front of Princess Alice. The triplets had learned that Princess Alice *did* know how to spray water on the crowd, so that trick was out. Bethany also knew that Princess Alice could turn in a circle and that she could awkwardly imitate a curtsy, balance on her rear feet, and more or less waltz around a perimeter as if she were in a circus ring. She had concluded to teach Princess Alice a new dance step, and because every weekend the Flynn family listened to the *Al Jolson Show* on the radio, Bethany had a tune stuck in her head from a recent program that would provide the best beat.

Slowly, deliberately, Bethany began to dance: step, kick-across; step, kick-across, watching Princess Alice intently for any sign that she was catching on. But Princess Alice just gave her a piercing look from her big eye and swept her trunk along the ground between the fences looking for pop-corn or other goodies.

Maybe she ought to add the tune, Bethany thought. She took a long breath and began singing, "Way down upon the Swan-ee River, far, far away." Step, kick-across; step, kick-across. An obnoxious little boy imitated her, screeching and high-kicking, but Bethany paid no attention to him.

"That's where my heart is turning ever ..." she sang. Step, kick-across.

Princess Alice yawned and sauntered over to check the far corner for treats. Bethany danced along to face her and kept singing. Princess Alice looked up.

Sucking in another long draught of the summer day, Bethany started over. No point in confusing matters by trying a different song, she decided. "Way down upon the Swan-ee River ..." Step, kick-across. Then just as doubt rose, Bethany was joined by a motherly looking woman who had picked up the tune and joined in, then by a short man to her left who sang in the tenor range. Hugo Stuka noticed the audience participation and began to clap his hands. Bethany shot him a grin and twirled to smile at the gathering group behind her, while she proceeded to dance with even more determination. Blood beat in her cheeks.

Then tears stung her eyes as to her amazement, Princess Alice took a long step to the left with her huge front foot. *Please!* Bethany prayed, although hardly believing it. The elephant's right leg kicked across in front to the left! The little crowd cheered. Bethany was too winded to continue singing but kept dancing as Hugo drew his harmonica from a pocket. Princess Alice danced along, keeping the beat. Bethany thought she could tell that the elephant was smiling. *Maybe!* When she lifted her hands above her head, shaking them in time to the tune, Princess Alice raised her trunk up and waved it from side to side, adding a trumpet blast that had the group cheering and drew other people over to join the crowd.

When the performance ended and the charmed zoo visitors began drifting away, Hugo circled around to exit through his narrow gate and came over to shake Bethany's hand. "I should hire you as my assistant," he said. "Good work."

"I have to show this to my sisters," she panted. "Will you play your harmonica again?"

"We have another hour or so before the zoo closes," Hugo said, glancing at his watch. "Otherwise your sisters will have to wait until tomorrow. But on Fridays we have bigger crowds, so tomorrow might not be good for dancing. Princess might be too distracted by the other people."

Bethany said she understood and ran for her bike. Pedaling south, she wasn't expecting the tenor to be trotting alongside her, but there he was, a wiry man with pinkish skin. "That was wonderful," he shouted. "You're a real entertainer. You're brave too. I like that."

Bethany smiled at him but kept going until she reached the curb. This was urgent. She didn't have much time to waste and was tempted to ride on across Thirteenth South and then pedal as fast as she could along Sixth East until she reached the alley, which she could cut through. But she was detained by the much-repeated rule that she had to walk her bike across any busy street. It would be just her luck to get hit by a car—or worse, someone in the family might see her ride across, and then she'd be in trouble. She hopped down, looking fast all three ways. *Good, no traffic.*

"Here, let me get your bike across the street for you," the tenor offered, reaching for the handlebars.

Was he still here? "No, thanks, I can manage," she said. But before she could prevent him, he had jumped onto Joyce's old bike and was riding it across the street by himself. Astounded, Bethany charged after him.

"Hey!" she yelled as he steered west, away from Sixth East. To her relief, he didn't ride very far, just to mid-block, where he took the bike up to a screened porch and propped it by the steps, then stood beside it smiling.

"Here you go. You know what? You need a glass of lemonade after all that singing."

Bethany shook her head. *Is he crazy?* she wondered.

Moments ago she had been ready to report him to Papa for stealing the bike. What would her sisters say if she came home without it? She couldn't imagine. Relieved, she stalked over to the porch, still breathing hard, and reached for the handlebars.

A broad, sweaty hand clamped over her mouth and an arm went around her waist. She found herself being hauled unceremoniously into the screened porch. Holding her fast, he jerked his elbow against the doorknob and opened into a dim, musty-smelling house and kicked the door shut.

Loosening a hand in order to lock up, he gave Bethany the opportunity to tear free and run in the other direction. *There must be a back door!* Then something clopped the side of her head and she went down, bumping against a cupboard. Before she knew it, he was *sitting* on her. She squinted, trying to focus her eyes while she caught her breath. Her head hurt.

"The others weren't half this much trouble," he muttered.

A hand appeared over her face. She kicked at him and grabbed for his hand, which was too big to bite and too flat to hold on to. She couldn't see more than a glimpse of her attacker through the hand that finally turned everything dark.

As they had dressed, then brushed one another's long hair, Annabel and Carolee assumed that Bethany must be helping with dinner. Joyce was playing the piano so loudly, it practically echoed upstairs. She hadn't been easy to be around, even after she moved back downstairs. The triplets had eavesdropped on discussions that turned on the specifics of Joyce's probation, her community service, and her being told she would not be allowed to partake of the sacrament, to know what serious trouble their sister was in and how severely she was being punished, yet they found it odd that daily life continued on as before. Papa started calling them the Talented Trio after they won second place in the ward show for their hobo dance. (Joyce complained that *she* had not been allowed to compete, with the implication that her Gershwin performance would have won the competition.)

Only after they heard Papa's voice and headed downstairs for supper did they realize that they had not seen Bethany or heard from her for quite a while. "I bet she's sneaked off to the park," Carolee said.

"But it's suppertime!" They did a quick reconnaissance of the house and yard. "Joyce's old bike is gone," Carolee noted. She and Annabel exchanged a nervous glance, then joined the rest of the family at the dining room table.

"Where's Bethany?" their mother asked distractedly.

Annabel shrugged and pulled out her chair so casually that the others took their places and allowed supper to begin. The questions continued until the two youngest admitted that the bicycle was gone.

"That's my bike!" Joyce protested.

Carolee pressed her lips together to keep from pointing out that it might be Joyce's bike, but she was prevented from even leaving the premises with it.

"Keep eating, everyone," Evan said. "I'll take a quick look around in the car. I'll be back in a jiffy," he said, sending Rose a reassuring look.

⸻

So much for supper, Evan thought. He drove to Fifth East with the windows down and the vents open, then proceeded slowly down the alley to Sixth East and into the park. There was not much question about where Bethany would go if she had decided to sneak off alone. From the center road, he could see that the zoo was closed. The evening crowd was clustering around the food stands and rides just outside the zoo. The food area was lit merrily in the deepening dusk.

Scanning toward the east, Evan saw the elephant trainer walking in the distance. His heart quickening, he turned his car through the parking area near the bandstand and cut a slow diagonal over the grass, watching for any signs of unrestrained children or dogs. Intercepting Stuka, who jumped, startled, Evan sprang out of the idling car.

Once Stuka saw who it was, he nodded and extended a hand. Evan thought his eyes seemed wary, but then the trainer was probably tired of being questioned as if he were a suspect. Evan tried to sound casual.

"We're missing Bethany, the blond one. Have you seen her this evening?"

"Earlier I saw her. Just Bethany, not her sisters."

Evan breathed easier. "You're sure? Bethany was here earlier?"

Stuka's weathered face crinkled into a grin. "I'm sure. She taught Princess a little dance." Then his look darkened. "She was hurrying home to get her sisters so they could see it, and they were supposed to be back before closing. They didn't make it in time. I promised Bethany I'd play my harmonica, this time for her sisters. You say she didn't come home?"

"Did you see her leave the park? Was she with anyone else?"

A pause. "No, no, I didn't see her leave. I had to clean up because the elephant was so excited from all the attention, she pooped a load." He extended a hand about knee-high.

"Mr. Stuka, did you see anyone who looked suspicious in that group around the elephant enclosure? Anyone hanging around? Maybe someone who paid more attention to Bethany than to your elephant?"

Stuka thought about it. "No, but quite a few people gathered to watch her dance with the elephant. I didn't notice anyone unusual. Everyone was clapping and—" He shook his head worriedly. "I would be glad to help you look for her."

Instead Evan had him write his address and telephone number again. "I'm relieved to know she was here so recently. Maybe we just missed each other in passing. Thanks."

Evan pulled onto the unpaved circle and drove back around, resisting the urge to radio for the cavalry. It was reassuring to know where Bethany had been an hour ago. Maybe she was home by now. If so, she would be in big trouble, but at least she would be home.

⚘

When her eyes opened, it was to more darkness. When she breathed in deeply, she smelled something bad.

"Beth-a-ny! Beth-a- ny!" Her name drifted faintly from

the distance, then closer by. A little way to her left, a pale rectangle framed a streetlight and her name floated again through what looked like a couple inches of air at the top of the window. *Was that Papa's voice?*

Here! I'm here! she tried to say through fabric that filled her mouth. She reached for the gag, but found her hands were tied to one side of her head. *I'm tied up!* She turned wildly and smacked her head into some wood. Running her forehead over it, she confirmed that there was a curved dusty feeling of wood and that her wrists were tied tightly together, anchored to the bedpost.

She uncurled her legs and realized her underpants were gone. She still wore her jumper and t-strap shoes, though. She was on something that must be a lumpy old bed. Here she was, gagged, her wrists tied up, and she was missing her underwear. *Why?*

The bicycle thief didn't seem to be anywhere nearby. The room smelled worse than a stink bug. She twisted her hands to try to work her wrists free. She wanted to see Mama and Papa. Tears wound down her cheeks as she realized how worried they'd be about her. She wanted to be home.

"Beth-a-ny!"

In a room below her, a radio came on. Bethany rubbed tears from her cheek with her upper arm. *Why a radio? Is he afraid of the dark?*

fifteen

Sol had disciplined himself to use only one lamp as he relaxed at night on his double bed and listened to the radio. That evening he had tucked the bicycle away in the shed behind the house and made sure there weren't any incriminating tracks marking his front yard. At least now he knew her name: *Bethany.* It burst through his bedroom window like a song. It was good that she could hear her folks calling for her—better than fine.

He flipped on a second lamp to see if, propping himself up on his right elbow, he could operate his magnetic toy with just his left hand. He managed to keep the spindle traveling in and out of the arc for four complete rounds, then let it drop and roll under the bed. He wasn't about to go after it. He giggled to think of how many magnetic wheels might be crouching under his bed.

A noise came from the upstairs storage space, so he turned the radio a notch louder. As far as he was concerned, the feisty lion cub could stew and fuss as much as she wanted to. Maybe later he would even take out the gag and free her wrists. Locked up, she couldn't get out. He had made sure the window was nailed shut a few inches down, which was too high for a child to get to. The trap door was secure in the kitchen, and that was the only way anyone could get in or out.

Why not leave her unbound after the search stopped for the night, he wondered. *A good idea*, he thought. Then she would really grasp the futility of trying to escape.

Meanwhile, she could access the bucket he had provided for her sanitary needs. He had even removed her underwear to make it easier. Not that he had planned to take her today. It was inconvenient, since he didn't have a packing crate ready. It was still in the shed and was blocked by the bicycle. No matter, as long as she was locked up. He felt weary after having baked in the sun at the park and then struggled to subdue this little princess. Let her poke around a bit, he thought, and scare herself into complete compliance. Eventually it would be time to play.

From his porch, he had seen her riding her bike to the park. Without really thinking about what he was doing, he had let instinct take over and followed her straight to the elephant, just as he expected. What a show she had put on with that dancing! It was too bad, really. It was a liability that so many people had seen her, but on the other hand, it made it a better challenge to subdue her with pills and tricks and go undetected by her cop father and his cohorts.

The rewards! he thought. This little golden-haired girl was not an unwashed waif like some of the neighbor children were. She was a real prize, who had been cared for like a precious blossom. *She's perfect!*

That's the word Ma used to use in reference to him. "It's fine if he stays my little boy forever," she had said to the doctor, who was concerned that he hadn't grown more. She bought him a Peter Pan costume and he went around the neighborhood in it on Halloween, long after the other boys his age had grown too big. It was about the time that Pa disappeared.

Now he loved collecting children, which was better than having animal pets. Children needed more food and exercise, but they were more amusing. This girly was pretty smart, but would be too innocent to know Sol was a child too, what with him being "undescended" and all that. Anyway, they had plenty of time to get acquainted, and then they could become friends—for a while anyway. No one expected pets to last forever.

He felt so cheered on by his success, so rejuvenated by it, that he flipped off the radio, fixed a tray, grabbed a flashlight, and went to the trap door.

⊶

"I think we should meet properly before we engage in any games," the bicycle thief said as he untied her. "Hello, Bethany. You can refer to me as your Most Gallant Knight. You are in an ancient castle. Did you see that I left you a bucket over there and some food and water?" He pointed with the flashlight. A rustling came from a different direction, but he paid no attention to it.

Bethany noticed the rustling and wondered if it was a rat! Her uppermost concern was whether the crazy bicycle thief wanted to kill her, but that did not seem to be the case. How could she be certain?

Humming, the gallant knight left again, taking the flashlight with him. Bethany felt her way in the dark, aided by some faint light that filtered in from the street. She urgently, if awkwardly, used the bucket, then took a drink of water from the old china cup. She sniffed the bowl and could tell it was applesauce. She thought the first heaping spoonful tasted wonderful, but the second bite was bitter. Leaving the remainder, proceeding cautiously in case there were rats, she explored the room. From below, the radio came on again and continued in its mindless merriment. *He plays it so loud. Don't the neighbors complain?*

The bad odor intensified as she shuffled over to what looked like the wardrobe but was not a wardrobe at all, it was two huge crates placed side by side. She edged around the corner of one of them and found a window-like opening. She peered inside and gasped to see half-open eyes looking back at her, blinking, then closing for good. The bad smell whooshed down her throat, and she teetered backward.

Trembling, she willed her legs over to the matching crate and looked farther down this time to spy a head of feathery light hair. There were no eyes peering upward. A warm puddle seeped from the bottom of the crate and soaked the soles of her t-straps. *No wonder the room smelled bad!* she realized.

This bicycle thief steals children! This must be Frankie—and Mary Agnes. Bethany stumbled backward, banging her hands and shins against unseen objects in the dark, and darted to the locked trap door, then stumbled toward the small, mostly closed window. Pressing her ear to it, she heard, behind the roar coming from the crickets outside, the sound of a car's motor, meaning that someone must be driving along Thirteenth South even though it was so late.

Is that another car? she screamed hoarsely until her voice entirely gave out. Downstairs the bicycle thief turned up the radio. She thought she heard Princess Alice's faint trumpeting.

She's locked up, too, Bethany thought. *Now we have that in common.* Shaking hard now, Bethany could not manage another sound from her throat. The children in the crates were not stirring. *Why don't they say something? Why don't they cry?*

She crept back to the bed and felt with one hand until she found her underpants. After she put them on, she felt safer. She crawled up the blanket to find the flat pillow. *Papa said there are men who hurt children in a way Mama didn't want him to talk about. The bicycle thief isn't that big, but he's pretty strong. Maybe he knows how to hurt children the way Papa meant.*

An image of the bicycle thief hauling a third crate up to the attic looped relentlessly in her mind. Her throat ached and her breath strained like a galloping horse. She felt her heart banging in her eardrums. She imagined her mother's voice saying *Bethany, you must calm down.*

Mama always said to think about something else, to think of something pleasant, when bad things happened. Bethany tried not to think about crate number three, or about Aunt Shirley not getting better after all they did for her to get well. She refused to figure out exactly how long Mary Agnes and Frankie had been hidden—all that time Papa and so many others had been searching for them. It was like the bicycle thief was a big spider that had wrapped its meals in silk cocoons in the attic, storing them for a later dinner.

She tried to imagine being home and crawling under the chenille covers with her sisters, a cool breeze creeping through their window. Sometimes her sisters' braids flipped and whipped her when they rolled over, but tonight she wouldn't mind if they did. She could tell how sweaty she smelled, the freshness of the bubble bath having melted away when she battled the bicycle thief. She tried to recall the scent of her sisters' hair after a bath and the way it felt when she helped fix their braids. She tried to believe Carolee and Annabel were lying on either side of her and Joyce and her parents were sleeping below.

If Carolee were here, she would think of a plan, she thought. *Annabel would hum a lullaby, but Carolee would do something. We are the alphabetical triplets. I am B for Bethany. I come in the middle where it's safe. No one can steal me from A and C.*

Another good thing was that in six months, Glenn and Margie's baby would be born. She tried to picture the baby and wondered whether it would be a boy or a girl. That led her to thinking of names. *Juliana, of course, if it's a girl.*

Lately she had wanted to play the Juliana game with her sisters to try out more names. *Natalie, for instance. Miranda or Arabesque.* She knew Annabel would say that arabesque is a piece of music and Carolee would say it's a dance step. *So what? Arabesque would be a wonderful name for a little girl.*

Bethany sighed. It was just as likely that Margie would have a boy, and boys' names were boring. *What else could she think about right now?* She remembered that she had been desperate to ride home and get her sisters. Hugo had promised to wait as long as he could. When she screamed, Princess Alice had trumpeted at her from her barn.

I have to show everyone Princess Alice's dance. Hey, I've completed my summer project! I've completed Annabel and Carolee's projects too, but they don't know it. I need to find a way out of here so I can show them. I need to tell them Princess Alice can dance and that the bicycle thief stole Frankie and Mary Agnes and me.

Restless again, she tossed in the heat. She used the bucket again. By morning, that bucket would smell really bad. She hated things that smelled bad. When she had made it back to the bed, all she could do was bury her face in the thin musty blanket. She considered raising a ruckus. *How can Mary Agnes and Frankie sleep like that? I'm exhausted, but I can't sleep at all. Maybe that bicycle thief got them drunk.*

Bethany remembered the bitter aftertaste to her apple-
sauce. *He wants to poison me—like Snow White. Well, maybe I should eat it and then I could sleep!* But she didn't want to be drugged if it meant she couldn't figure out how to escape. She thought some more about it and decided that the next time he appeared at the trap door, she would kick his jaw hard and slide past him through the opening. Maybe she could run fast enough to unlock one of the doors.

No, she decided. Her chances of success were slim. He could grab her ankle and she would fall flat like Joyce did with the fishing line. *Maybe I can scare him by telling him my sister is a criminal. I'll tell him Papa is a detective. I'll get Mary Agnes and Frankie to help. We'll promise him we won't tell.* But what if another child disappeared, would she be able to keep silent? It didn't seem likely that he would believe them in any case.

She imagined her father's car pulling up at the curb. She pictured Papa and his partner banging on the front door. Hoarse or not, she could scream through the crack in the window. She could scream until her throat burst. If anyone came along the street tomorrow, she would scream and pound the window until they heard. *But if I do, he'll tie me up and gag me.*

She closed her eyes and breathed through her mouth. With all her energy, she pictured Princess Alice crashing through the locked door and stomping the bicycle thief into his linoleum. She colored this scene for a long time in the recesses of her mind until she faded into a restless half-sleep and dreamed of strange things at Liberty Park. In her dream, she still sang: "Way down upon the Swan-ee River, far, far away." She could see herself dancing: step, kick-across; step, kick-across.

A call to the farm confirmed Bethany had not found her way there. Glenn and Margie rushed back to help look for her. Once it grew too late for the officers and volunteers to be hollering up and down residential streets, they began combing Liberty Park. Eventually everyone's legs and voices gave out, so they called it a night and agreed to meet outside the zoo entrance early the next morning.

Evan, on the other hand, did not give up the search. For one thing, he could not bear to see the terror in Rose's eyes. He drove through the neighborhood until dawn, running possibilities through his exhausted mind. He had interviewed Hugo again and his wife, Anna. They seemed honest and very concerned about Bethany, but Hugo had never been officially cleared in the disappearances of Frankie and Mary Agnes. Evan's partner wanted to get a search warrant, but Evan had argued there wasn't any evidence for that.

Back at the park, he eased his car over to the unpaved circle toward Thirteenth South when he spotted the girl who exercised horses. *Nora, that was her name.* Careful not to spook the horse this time, he braked and got out of the car. He had never felt so weary or desperate.

"Good morning, Nora."

"Hello. What's going on? There are police everywhere. Don't tell me there's another missing kid."

"I'm afraid this time it's my daughter," he said, trying to conceal his fear. He showed her a recent photograph of Bethany dancing in a talent show with her sisters. "She's in the center."

Nora studied it, then ruefully shook her head.

Heartsick, he turned away.

She touched his sleeve. "Something odd, though, this morning," she said. "Probably nothing."

"What's that?"

"As I rode past Fourth East, I heard a radio playing pretty loud for this time of the morning. Once I got close, it shut off and I couldn't hear anything. Everything went back to being really still."

Evan thought about it. Though busy, the neighborhood was always quiet early in the morning, and he didn't believe in coincidences. "Exactly where was that? Do you know?"

She took an agonizing few seconds to orient herself, then pointed across Thirteenth South. "Back that way a bit, not inside the park, but close by it." She gazed at the homes across the street and saw the girl in the wheelchair already being pushed across her lawn. "Those people are up early! Maybe the radio woke them, although I don't think it was next door to them."

"It was probably the commotion from the search that kept them awake," Evan said, wondering guiltily if it would affect Lara's health.

Suddenly Nora's horse shied and reared, and instinctively Evan ducked away from its hooves. As Nora fought to regain control, something huge and gray hurtled past them, running silently.

"It's Princess Alice!" Nora said. "She's out again. Poor Hugo."

Sure enough. There was Stuka hustling down Sixth East on foot, trying to catch up. The elephant dodged a patrol car turning into the park, then she crossed the street and headed for the houses as if recruited for a mission. Trotting past a screened porch at mid-block, Princess Alice turned in at the far side of the house.

"Come on, Jackpot, I guess we can do it again," Nora said.

She reined her horse around and left at a gallop. Evan felt hope kick in like the adrenaline streaming into his blood.

Bethany was last seen with that elephant! he recalled. As he ran toward the street, Evan heard glass shatter and wood rip.

First, Bethany saw a weak light, then a long gray arm bashing through the window. The arm retreated, and then its fingers tore the frame apart, leaving a jagged hole. The arm swept inside the space, searching for something, almost like an elephant's trunk. *My gosh, it is an elephant's trunk!*

Bethany grabbed for it, as if she were living out her favorite daydream. The trunk clamped around her waist and pulled her into the outside air. Down she slid to Princess Alice's head, feeling the hairy gray skin of the animal's neck. She grabbed onto the elephant's soft ears and tightened her knees to keep herself from falling off. *I'm free!* she realized.

Shouts! Running feet!

The bicycle thief burst around the corner of his house. Princess Alice straightened her trunk and roared. Bethany screamed as she felt the elephant's great muscles tighten beneath her. Afraid that Princess would charge that nasty man with her aboard, she held on tight to avoid getting tossed off.

The bicycle thief fell back and stared at the elephant, his jaw agape, but Princess Alice stood her ground. Police cars were pulling up onto the lawns like it was a parking lot.

Finally! Bethany thought. She called out, shouting "they're inside!" to the officers who, one after another, charged out of their cars. "Mary Agnes and Frankie are in the attic. The trap door is above the kitchen!"

Several of the officers ran onto the porch. A few of them

approached the bicycle thief, who seemed about to run but then straightened up and said, "You're parked on my lawn."

"He did it!" Bethany yelled. "He stole us. Frankie and Mary Agnes are upstairs in crates."

The officers closed in on him.

Bethany realized that Hugo was standing beside her, panting. He raised a hand to the elephant's shoulder and shook his head at the glass and wood splinters on the ground. Bethany noticed that Hugo looked different, seeing him from above. Everyone looked different from that vantage.

She spotted her father. Poor Papa looked exhausted. She waved her arms and shouted uncontrollably, she was so thrilled to know she would be going home with him now. He ran toward her, grinning and wiping away tears.

Papa isn't afraid of Princess Alice any more than I am! she realized. "He stole me, Papa!" she cried, pointing to the bicycle thief, who was being handcuffed. "He hid me upstairs with Mary Agnes and Frankie."

Emotions hit Evan like a succession of waves—relief, excitement, outrage, fury. He whirled around toward the suspect and lunged at him; a fellow officer grabbed his arm to restrain him and another pulled the suspect away toward a police car, Sol's feet barely touching the ground. Evan rubbed his hands over his face and fought to regain composure.

"Good morning, Bethany," he managed.

She bounced a bit—bounced on the elephant's head! "Good morning, Papa. Princess Alice found me!"

"So I see." He nodded to Hugo and stretched trembling arms toward his daughter, but Bethany shook her head no. She had earned her spot on the elephant and was going to stay there for the moment.

The other missing children—what about them? he remembered. And he had to call Rose. He looked up at Bethany and said, "Don't go anywhere." It seemed so unnecessarily absurd that they both laughed. Evan bounded up the porch steps and pushed through the door.

Bethany figured that both she and Princess Alice might be in trouble for being where they shouldn't, so she was relieved that Papa didn't seem angry. Surely the policemen's noses would lead them to Mary Agnes and Frankie, she thought. One thing about grown-ups was that eventually they sorted everything out. Pretty soon she would find her way down from the elephant into Papa's arms, and they would be on their way home to Mama and her sisters. Wait until they heard that she had solved all three summer projects in one night! Carolee could read about it all in the newspaper!

Bethany reminded herself to tell Papa that Joyce's old bicycle must be hidden somewhere, but she was so distracted by the exuberant girl who had ridden over on horseback, that she quickly forgot to mention it. Grinning, the girl waved at Bethany and dismounted to kneel beside the thin girl who had been brought over in a wheelchair.

The police officers looked happy and were slapping each other on the back and shaking Hugo's hand, as Hugo tried to shoo away a man with the camera. The police acted as if they—not Princess Alice—had solved this gigantic case. A fire engine arrived. Bethany laughed, wondering if it was for her. Did they think she needed a ladder to climb down? She felt as if she were in a circus, there was so much going on all at the same time. She couldn't take it all in. Best of all was the feeling that she was free—and here she was, personally sitting on Princess Alice!

She laughed and waved at everyone until she saw an officer

emerge from the house carrying Frankie wrapped in a blanket. At that, Bethany started to cry. Another officer led a dazed and bedraggled Mary Agnes by the shoulders. A woman shrieked and ran toward the girl. Flashbulbs popped nearby. Princess Alice squealed. Bethany stroked the elephant's head, and Hugo spoke a command into her near ear as the flashbulbs flared again.

Suddenly, amid all the tumult, Bethany felt supremely content, even more content than she would that evening when she'd eat brownies in bed with her sisters. She leaned forward, planting her chin against the back of the elephant's head, stroking the soft, fan-like ears and kissing its prickly head. Likely, these minutes on board Princess Alice would never return.

"Thank you for stealing me back," she whispered. "I adore you, Princess Alice-Arabesque."

At that cue from her circus days, the elephant squeaked and sent a shimmy the full length and breadth of her body. Bethany tightened her grip, and Princess Alice began to dance like before: step, kick-across; step, kick-across.

Epilogue

Princess Alice moved into the shade on the northwest part of her corral, away from the conversation Hugo was having with the other zookeepers. As they spoke, they did not know that she saw the pictures in their minds: a larger barn, a wider corral, a companion elephant. It had been decades since she had been with others of her kind.

Hugo, who knew her best, had talked every day of this new place. Princess knew that soon another huge truck would back up to her barn and load her into it and that this time she would not protest. It had been a nice run at Liberty Park, especially the secret baths and periodic jaunts through the neighboring streets. She did not want to move. She knew she could break any chain or split any truck, but that finally it wouldn't matter. Even a princess had to bow to the inevitable sometimes.

She still remembered her childhood when she migrated with her herd for better food and fresh water. She had not forgotten her capture and separation from her family. She could still see the zoo where she met Hugo, the circus they joined, the deceitful manager who had bartered away her calves. Vividly, she remembered those funny little creatures that had emerged from her with their unstable bearing, the way they nursed, and how she guarded them and mourned each one, especially the calf she had rolled over on, which had bleated so pitifully at her feet.

She thought of the human child who had danced with her and screamed for Princess to rescue her. She remembered how she had lifted her out of the attic and away from that scary little man. She thought it was a strange balance interacting with humans. They brought her food, kept her warm, nursed her aches, and loaded her onto trucks, but very few of them understood her. None of them understood her as much as she understood them.

Now it was almost time to surrender this shady home of sixteen years and let them take her to the new zoo by the mountains. She would not promise to be well-behaved once she got there, depending on what she encountered, and already she imagined tearing through the vivid gardens and raining flowers down on people. She needed to remind the zoo keepers of her power, but she would capitulate like she always had without hurting anyone. It would be fun, and afterward she would return to her enclosure to eat her supper, saluting the next morning by cooling herself off with a refreshing shower and the same for anyone near her.

The way she imagined it was how it came to be. Hugo led her into the truck. She grumbled a bit but allowed herself to be moved and secretly approved of her new home. For more than a decade, she reigned over the Hogle Zoo and its enchanted crowds. When she did not wake one morning, an artist inscribed her visage in stone, along with her name. Princess Alice would not be forgotten. That was enough.

The Real Princess Alice

As documented in the following news clippings, Princess Alice stayed two years at Liberty Park beginning in 1916, followed by fifteen years at Hogle Zoo. She had a calf, Prince Utah, that lived eleven months and was sometimes called Prince Charming or simply Pat.

"Dutch" Shider trustingly lies beneath his 4.5-ton charge. Alice had another trainer as well, Harry Petchell. The fictional character of Hugo Stuka conflates aspects of the two men.

Wanderlust Seizes City's Pachyderm

Princess Alice, Tiring of Hard Work, Goes on Rampage, Terrorizing Women.

PRINCESS ALICE, the city's pet elephant at the Liberty park zoo, went rampaging yesterday afternoon. As if scenting the atmosphere of her jungle habitat, Alice went on strike from her task of pulling tree stumps at the park and gamboled off for a little outing. Frightened at the bark and snap of dogs at her heels, the giant pachyderm plunged through barns, sheds, fences and over ditches like a British "tank."

While women fled from their homes with children as the elephant entered their yards, sweeping down fences and trees with her great bulk, Alice swung her long proboscis contentedly over her head as if she were having the time of her life. Before she was recaptured three hours later a mile up Big Cottonwood canyon, portions of Sugar House resembled the wake of an invading host.

Amused at the spectacle of the trumpeting monster, hundreds of men and boys followed in her path. Keepers almost had her stopped several times when a yelping dog would rush out and join the howling canine tribe at her heels. This spurred her to more furious flight and shorter crosscuts through yards and fields. Sheds and outhouses were splintered under her tons of weight, and one barn collapsed in a heap as she tore through the door. Emerging from under the lumber wreckage of the structure, Alice trumpeted a warning and proceeded up Twelfth South street.

Herman H. Greene, commissioner of parks and public property, took up the chase of the city's pet in a police machine. Men tugged vainly at hooks in her trunk, while others tried to scatter the fast increasing tribe of dogs.

She continued up the road until she came to the trestle work of the county silica beds. There she halted when confronted by a perpendicular incline. Further progress was impossible and she turned around and met her pursuers good naturedly.

Harry Petchell, Alice's former trainer with a circus, mounted her head and rode her back to the park. Her legs and trunk were badly lacerated from contact with barbed wire fences and buildings. At no time was she vicious. She was docility itself when returned to her domicile. S. R. Lambourne, superintendent of parks, sent several employees over the elephant's trail to repair the damage.
—*Salt Lake Herald*, Nov. 15, 1916

Princess Alice Has Semiannual Bath; Lampblack Is Soap

Pachyderm Rubbed Down With Oil; Manicuring Next on Program.

Princess Alice had her semiannual bath today and now the lady is spic and span as could be possible. Her skin virtually shines as though she had just finished a good scrubbing at the hands of a corps of Spartan shoe shiners.

Lamp black and oil instead of soap and water were the unusual constituents of Alice's bath and she wasn't preparing for a black face act at that.

Of course Princess Alice—as everyone knows—is the elephant at Liberty park zoo. She only takes a bath every six months—that's just a habit of elephants—but it is a very important event in an elephant's life. Can you imagine yourself lathered with a mixture of lampblack and oil every six months?

"Dutch" Shider, Alice's trainer, was in charge of the bathing ceremony today and, aided by a corps of park attendants, started in early this morning. It was almost evening before their task was finished.

To begin with, the young lady—Alice is yet in her teens from an elephantine standpoint of speaking—was chained to a tree and ladders placed on either side. Shider climbed up one ladder and Dave Adams the other. With huge sponges they started to scrub her down with the lampblack and oil mixture. This required three hours and afterward Alice was taken out in the bright sunlight today.

"Now Alice is ready for the winter with one exception," announced Dutch after completing the bath.

"All she needs now is a manicuring and I guess we will have to wait until I can find some blacksmith to make us a pair of cast iron manicuring files and a hickory orange stick."—*Salt Lake Telegram*, Nov. 10, 1916

ALICE BRINGS TRUNK FOR THREE-DAY STAY WITH SALT LAKE KIDS

Grownups Can Make Youngsters Happy by Joining Club of Princess and Giving Dollar for Each Dime Donated.

Cover Bets of the Tots Takes but a Dollar

✧ ✧ ✧ ✧ ✧ ✧ ✧ ✧ ✧ ✧ ✧ ✧ ✧

Fifteen hundred Salt Lakers can make 25,000 children happy by joining the Princess Alice Dollar club. The idea is for each one of the 1500 to cover the bet of one Salt Lake youngster. Fifteen hundred dimes have been staked on Princess Alice by Salt Lake kiddies. A dollar on top of each one of those dimes will keep Princess Alice in Salt Lake.

Princess Alice Dollar Club.
            Care of Salt Lake Telegram.
    Sign me on the rolls of the Princess Alice Dollar club.
I   inclose $ _____   to   cover   the   bet   of
_____, Salt Lake youngster.

Princess Alice, the big mama elephant of the Sells-Floto circus, came to Salt Lake bright and early this morning, to the delight of every child in town. Fifteen hundred kiddies had more than a passing interest in her arrival because they have staked their dimes on her and the want her to live here always.

If the people of Salt Lake get behind the movement launched with such vim by their sons and daughters, there is no doubt but that Princess Alice will be a permanent resident of Liberty park. Whether she is purchased or not she is going to stop off here for three days and visit with the Salt Lake kiddies.

THE TELEGRAM made arrangements today with the owners of the Sells-Floto circus to break Alice's contract with the show and let her stay in Salt Lake until Monday. Now if the good people of Salt Lake come forward and aid the children, Alice will be permitted to jump her contract and quit the show business forever.

She will be left in Salt Lake until Monday, while the circus goes to Provo and Logan. If the remainder of the purchase price is raised by Monday, Alice will be left here as a perpetual delight for Salt Lake children and an everlasting attraction for Liberty park.

Sixteen hundred dollars has been raised for the purchase of Princess Alice.

Thousands of Salt Lake young- sters have been in constant communication with THE TELEGRAM, urging aid in bringing Princess Alice to Zion. The Elephant Editor has heard their hopes expressed over the telephone, in personal visits and letters sent to the office. That they are sincere in their desire for an elephant for Liberty park, is evidenced in the manner in which they have given of their own funds.

Fifteen hundred Salt Lake youngsters have sent their dimes to the Elephant Editor to help pay for Princess Alice.

Some outside aid has been given them and the fund now totals $1600.

That is not enough. The youngsters need a little more aid from the grownups of Salt Lake. Salt Lake has thousands of men and women who can aid. They can cover these fifteen hundred dimes with dollars, and not miss it half as much as the kiddies missed their dimes. Just think of the oodles of candy, chewing gum, peanuts, ice cream and other childhood delicacies that have been laid upon the altar of this elephant!

That in itself shows that they want Princess Alice.

Now, right here in Salt Lake, there are thousands of men who would give a dollar to make a kid happy.

The Princess Alice Dollar Club will give them the opportunity.

The object of this club is to make kids happy.

THE TELEGRAM wants the elephant in Liberty park because the youngsters of Salt Lake want her there.

THE TELEGRAM believes that there are more than 1500 men and women in Salt Lake who, like THE TELEGRAM, want to make the boys and girls of this city happy.

If 1500 Salt Lakers will give a dollar each, to cover the dimes laid down by the kiddies, then this fund is assured. Surely the grownup can lay down ten dimes for every one laid down by the children under 12 years of age.

That is the object of the Princess Alice Dollar club.

It only takes a dollar to join, and each membership is good for tons of satisfaction in the knowledge that the dollar went to add to the happiness of 25,000 Salt Lake children and paved the way for more pleasure for the children that are to come to this fair city in the future.

Prospective members of the Princess Alice Dollar club will have to hurry, or it will be too late.

The big princess will be here until Monday. If those 1500 dimes are covered before, she will be here forever. The short and quick action is that the dollars must come before that day, or Princess Alice will be on the road.

The Dollar Club Editor will take care of the money, and if those dimes are matched the total fund for the benefit of Princess Alice will be turned over to the city on Monday. —*Salt Lake Telegram*, Aug. 25, 1916

ALICE MUST PAY ROOM RENT

✧　✧　✧　✧　✧　✧　✧　✧　✧　✧　✧　✧

Liberty Park Pet Will Be Used as
Source of Power for Heavy Work

✧　✧　✧　✧　✧　✧　✧　✧　✧　✧　✧　✧

ELEPHANT "MOTOR TRUCK"

The delicacies that are given to Princess Alice by the children of the city, the peanuts, pieces of cake, cantaloupes, watermelons, apple pie, etc., are free to her, but not so her board and lodging from the city. She must pay for that.

While the park department is making provision that Alice shall be kept warm and well fed through the winter months, it is also preparing to make her pay. "Dutch" Snyder, the trainer of Alice, is busy building for her a gigantic harness.

When the harness has been completed the park will be virtually supplied with a motor truck that is run by a brain instead of by gasoline. If there is anything heavy to be hauled from one part of the park to the other, Alice will be the source of motive power. If there is land in the park to be plowed for planting, Alice will pull the plow. If there are heavy objects to be lifted, the strength of Alice will serve instead of some heavy and much slower piece of machinery.

Recently Sidney Lambourne, superintendent of parks, had an object lesson in the vast strength of which the elephant is possessed. The trainer caused the elephant to put its head against the back of Mr. Lambourne's big six-cylinder automobile. With the engine reversed and running on full power, the car was unable to hold back the elephant. Princess Alice shoved the car ahead without difficulty, though the back wheels were spinning in reverse action.

Such strength appealed to the park superintendent as being an asset and, after a conference had been held with Alice's keeper, the material for the harness was bought and work upon its construction was immediately begun.
—*Salt Lake Telegram*, Sept. 25, 1916

His Highness' Nurse Is Driven Dotty by Queries

Yesterday was questionnaire day at Liberty park. Everyone wanted to know how Princess Alice and her little baby elephant, Prince Charming, who was left by the stork early in the morning, were getting along. "Dutch" Schider, whose anxiety has prevented him having a good sleep since June, 1916, says that if the spectators don't quit asking questions he'll have to go to Provo.

A reporter asked a few questions. "Dutch" answered most of them as follows:

"What is it?" "A boy, of course."

"How's the missus?" "Doing nicely."

"Does she feed it?" "You bet!"

"How often?" "Just one meal after another."

"How does it drink?" "With its mouth."

"What does it do with its nose?" "What d'ye think he does with it?"

"How long will it be a baby?" "Three years."

"Why can't we see it?" "Because he's too young and his mother might object."

"When can we see it?" "Just as soon as the weather will permit; maybe Saturday or Sunday."

"What's it worth?" "Ten thousand dollars; Sells-Floto have offered $5000 for him if he attains the age of 6 months."

"Say, Dutch, if a Red Cross ram sells at auction for thousands of dollars, what will a baby elephant bring?"

But the receiver had been hung up. —*Salt Lake Herald*, Apr. 30, 1918

YOUNG PRINCE RUNS AWAY AT LIBERTY PARK

Mother Hard to Comfort Until Her Offspring Is Brought Back

His royal nibs, Prince Utah, the prize baby elephant of all time, is growing obstreperous.

Perhaps it's the hot weather that is making "Pat" feel so gay and festive these days. At any rate, the pride of Salt Lake is getting to be as lively as a Winter Garden chorus girl. He's keeping "Dutch" Shider, the big mogul of the city zoo, on edge with his capers, and his royal mother, Princess Alice, in daily fear and trembling for his safety.

"Pat" was particularly gay yesterday and badly afflicted with that somewhat common summer ailment, wanderlust. He didn't want to stay put at all and objected strenuously to the narrow confines of the elephant enclosure in Liberty park.

"Dutch" nipped several abortive attempts of the princeling to break out of the enclosure, but the wily "Pat" watched his opportunity and when the trainer was away for a moment made a wild dash for the great beyond, the great outdoors, or whatever lay beyond the enclosure ropes. He succeeded, too, in breaking through and was bound for "somewhere in Salt Lake" when the big mother's wild trumpeting brought "Dutch" rushing to the scene of the getaway.

And maybe you don't think Princess Alice was cutting some capers herself about that time. She must have had visions of a lost son and heir, for she sure behaved scandalously. Trumpeting wildly, she made a grand sally after the absconding "Pat." Stakes were uprooted and it looked for a moment as though Liberty park and everything in the near vicinity was doomed.

"Dutch," however, arrived on the scene just in time to nip "Pat's" plans for a day off in the bud and to restore him to his, by this time, thoroughly alarmed mother. He saved the day and probably prevented wholesale destruction of buildings and trees by bringing the runaway back to the enclosure before Princess Alice had fully broken her bonds.

All of which goes to show that the big elephant is some fond of her offspring and that it's going to be a bad ninth inning for anyone with effrontery enough to try to take "Pat" away from her. She's as proud of Prince Utah as any human mother might be of her first born and when it comes to cuddling and all that sort of thing—well, the youngster down Liberty park way gets his share and then some. —*Salt Lake Herald*, Aug. 5, 1918

"This is a charming story, deliciously nostalgic but with a hard edge of causes and consequences. Since so much of the story is told from the point of view of children or teens (the alphabetical triplets are a marvelous device), it has a different tone and new perspective for Linda, whose novels and short stories have previously dealt with adult protagonists and cultures ranging from Native Americans to the inner world of serial killers. For a time, Linda lived just minutes from Liberty Park, and her celebration of its earlier history (and mystery) evokes a period and place in Salt Lake City that gets bumped over too easily.

"My favorite scene is where Bethany teaches the elephant, Princess Alice, to dance. The elephant is key in the story—not in a *deus ex machina* way but in evoking the mysterious and magical, as other aspects of the animal world do, and the world of children. Elements like Shirley's death, the real-world consequences of Glenn's and Marjorie's youthful sexual experimentation, the chilling *modus operandi* of the kidnapper, and Joyce's obvious amorality prevent us from seeing this as sentimental. Linda has written a story for all of us—adults and children alike—but especially for those who have ever lived in and loved Salt Lake City."

—Lavina Fielding Anderson, past president, Association for Mormon Letters

"This is a delightful tale of mystery, kidnappings, and elephants. Linda has crafted a fine story, with interesting characters, particularly Princess Alice, the first elephant I saw as a boy. I also have a great interest in elephants, which was stirred by Joseph Smith's mention of them in the Jaredite culture. As an interesting sidebar, the two elephants Joseph envisioned sailing to America would have required approximately 110,000 lbs. of fodder (55 tons) to satisfy the average daily need of 150 lbs. per elephant. Plus, those critters are a thirsty bunch. Drinking 50 gallons of water would require a massive storage tank of 37,000 gallons for the two. The water would have weighed 292,000 lbs. (146 tons). The total weight of this food and water for the one-year voyage would have been slightly more than 200 tons. Did Joseph mention that the ancient ship was well buttressed? What an imagination that man had!"

—Richard Van Wagoner, Signature Books board member, written for Signature Books in August 2010, two months before his own death in October

"*Thieves of Summer* is not a sleekly engineered thriller with the usual slot-and-filler characters ticking along from chill to chill. It was not made as a roller coaster ride, designed by some poker-faced Newtonian to keep you off-balance, half out of the car, often upside-down, until delivering you shaken and perhaps nauseated, hands in the air, to a platform where you started—a finale which you didn't even want to see coming. No, this story shows you all the cards, presents everyone as neighbors, and investigates the neighborhood you live in, not some other place. It is a story of real people involved in sin, who also happen to have among them an amazing elephant that remembers what it was like being wild (and has the mischievous manner of an adolescent girl). The humans too are sometimes wild, sometimes wanton, but live in a community that wants to help them outgrow all that. It is a community anchored in love, afloat despite all the forces that could destroy it."

—DENNIS CLARK was one of Linda's colleagues in a writers' group that included Levi Peterson, Bruce Jorgensen, and—after Linda moved to Arizona—Eugene England, John and Karla Bennion, and Tim Slover. Dennis is the author of *Tinder: dry poems* and *rough stone, rolling waters* and editor with Eugene England of *Harvest: Contemporary Mormon Poetry*